MW00613395

The
Bid
Catcher

Anita Davis

This is a work of fiction. Names, characters, businesses, places, events and incidents are either the products of the author's imagination or used in a fictitious manner. Any resemblance to actual persons, living or dead, or actual events is purely coincidental.

Copyright © 2019 Anita Davis

All Rights Reserved. No part of this publication may be reproduced, stored in a retrieval system, or transmitted, in any form or in any means – by electronic, mechanical, photocopying, recording or otherwise – without prior written permission.

ISBN-10: 1-946721-10-7
ISBN-13: 978-1-946721-10-5

Books may be purchased in quantity by contacting the author Anita Davis:
Set Apart Publishing
PO Box 39229
Chicago, IL 60639
or by email at authoranitadavis@gmail.com

ACKNOWLEDGMENTS

As always, I'd like to thank my betas, critique partners, and Book Euphoria Babes for indulging my apprehensions but provide solid and valuable feedback and encouragement. I love all y'all.

To the readers who follow me from book to book and indulge my style of writing. You each doeth my heart merry. ***insert kissy face***

To my return readers and those who may be reading my work for the first time because of this collaboration, hope that with each paperback page turned or kindle page flipped, you each enjoy the story more and more.

1

"Hey, ma."

"Don't hey me. When are you coming home again? And who told you to move away anyway?"

Jeremy chuckled as he stopped cutting up bell peppers to give his mother more of his attention. "Ma, I've been gone from home for like fifteen years. You should be used to it by now."

"Lil boy, don't sass me. I asked you a question, now answer it."

He could only chuckle as he got back to cutting the bell peppers to put in his special marinara sauce. "I'll be home soon enough to see your pretty face, lady."

Although she wanted to continue to badger him about coming to visit her again, she paused, blushing. No matter how far away he lived from in Chicago, him calling her "pretty" always made her feel so close to him.

"Ma, you still there?"

"Yeah." She sniffled. She had helped many boys mature into men over the years as a foster mother, but Jeremy Brighton, the one she was finally able to give birth to when she was forty-one and her late husband, Harold, was forty-five, always brought her the greatest joy with mere words.

They didn't think they would ever have any children of their own, but God had shown them that He worked in his own time and not on their desired schedule.

Jeremy had brought so much joy to her life and pain. Not mischievous pain, but the pain of a mother having to accept the fact that their child was grown and going off to college. She didn't want to be an empty nester, so Jeremy further annoyed her once he graduated from San Diego Culinary Institute and decided to stay in the new city he'd become familiar with.

She had hoped that he would move back to Chicago and be closer to her. And like he said, he'd been gone from home for close to fifteen years, but that didn't make his absence any easier on her.

And being the private and stubborn man he always had been, she knew the next question she was going to ask him wouldn't go over so well with him. But that's where her motherly skills were sure to come in. She knew she was pretty much going to have to force him to do what she needed him to do.

"Jeremy, I need your help."

He chuckled wondering what could thee Peaches Brighton need his help for. With as many people that she had helped over the years, she always had someone willing and able to assist her. Not to mention the buttery way she said his name, he knew she was up to something. "Ma, if it's moving furniture or something, why don't you just ask Kadaris to come over and do it for you?"

"Did I say I needed some furniture moved? Did I say *what* I needed just yet?" Her tone came out clipped as she held the card in her hand in midair, stopping her game of solitaire. Her fine lips tightened, her light brown eyes narrowed, and she looked ahead of her as if he was in front of her and would be able to see the glaring stare she was sending him.

"No ma'am." With the tightness in her voice, he quieted his laughter, already knowing how she was looking at him on the other end of the phone.

"I'm not on the phone with Kadaris, I'm on the phone with you and I said I need *your* help."

"Okay, Ma. What is it that you need my help with?"

"You have to say yes, first."

He didn't hide his laughter this time. He chuckled loudly right before saying, "No ma'am. You know that's not how it works between us. I love you with all my heart, but there's just some stuff you know I'm not down for. But that's also why God blessed you with all your foster kids over the years. Between all of us, you're always taken care of."

She shook her head. "Again, I'm not talking to them, I'm talking to the one where when I was forty-one years old, I labored for sixteen painful hours before his peanut head made its grand entrance into the world."

"I love you too." He smiled.

She smiled. "Oh, hush. Just say yes to what I'm asking."

"Momma, no. But what are you trying to get going this time? And with the way you're carrying on about it, bringing up the infamously long labor story, it's starting to sound like it's really big. Add on to that, you're trying to get me to agree to it without first telling me about it. What are you up to lady?" He paused his musing in his kitchen. "I bet Ms. Geraldine is in on it too, isn't she? Is she sitting there next to you? Hey, Ms. Geraldine," Jeremy said loud into his phone hoping she could hear him if she was indeed near his mother.

His bright smile widened thinking about the two best friends who were always in cahoots with one another.

Rather than continuing to beat around the bush with him, Mama Peaches decided to put it all out there. "Well, you know that the neighborhood is not as glorious as it used to be." Her normally strong voice wavered. "Geraldine, I, and many others around the neighborhood have been asking the city to help us get the necessary funds to buy these abandoned homes and businesses so that they can be rented out to our kind. We want to get back the valor and beauty it once had. Get it back to looking like the reason why your father and I settled in this neighborhood in the first place."

Jeremy's humor sobered up at the mention of his father. He wasn't sure if she would recount how her father was able to pay for their house, in full, within the first two years of being in it. While the story made him full of pride and was a testament to the kind of man Harold Brighton was, the fact that he was no longer there to share the story himself and was always referred to in the past tense stirred him. He really did miss his dad.

Her beckoning voice brought him out of his memories of his father. "Jeremy," her face reddened, "you know the city of Chicago didn't give us any monies to fix this place up but rather directed us to a few organizations that could. Well, Geraldine and I worked hard to convince those companies to give as much money as they did, but we still need more."

"Ma, I wish I could, but it sounds like you need millions or something close to that. I know I do good for myself, but not that good."

"See, this ain't even about money, Bubba."

He shook his head before dropping it. She had called him by his childhood nickname. She really meant business when she called him that.

"Bubba, I need those good looks of yours your daddy and I passed down to you."

He coughed up a nervous laugh. "What?"

"Yes. Geraldine and I figured that with all of the handsome boys I helped turn into men over the years, y'all could do your parts in paying it forward to the neighborhood."

His forehead scrunched as he blurted out, "So you want to get the money from all of us?"

"Bubba, this ain't about your money, it's about your looks. Geraldine and I want to put on a bachelors auction starring you guys as the bachelors."

Grateful that he was a master chef could handle his knife in calm or chaotic times, he still dropped his knife and blinked rapidly. "Say what now, Peaches?"

"Boy, don't make me reach through this phone and slap you for calling me by my name." She cocked her head. She stared amidst, hoping his memory would know just what deadpan look she was serving him at the moment.

He chuckled. "Ma, sorry, but I really had to stop you. Me, get up in front of strangers as a bachelor? It's like you haven't met me before."

"Oh, I've met you. I know you and how you are and that's why I'm no longer asking you to be a bachelor. I'm telling you, you're going to be one." She slammed the two of spade down on a three of diamonds in a row of her solitaire game.

"So you don't want me to ever come back home then?" He chuckled.

"You weren't always so quiet and kept to yourself." She huffed. "You sure can be a knucklehead at times."

Ignoring what had caused the change she mentioned. He laughed harder than he had up to that point. "Ma, you act like you forgot that I don't do crowds. I'm a loner. That's why cooking is perfect for me. Aside from talking to the staff under me at the restaurant, I just stick to my skillet. Nothing new here."

"Bubba, please do this for your dear momma." She knew he could hear the pout in her voice, even though he couldn't see the downward curved lips. "One of the organizations said that whatever we can raise on our own, they'll exponentially multiply their contribution to it. They just want to see our efforts."

"Ma, Bubba loves you with all his heart." He laughed referring to himself in the third person. "Again, you know something like this is not my style, but I know with how relentless you and Ms. Geraldine are, y'all will definitely come up with the money needed to fix the neighborhood how you want it to be."

"Je-"

He cut off her ensuing rant. "I love you ma, but I

really have to go. Talk to you again soon." He ended the call before she could get in another word. He knew she would only continue to hound him on the matter if he stayed on the phone with her.

Besides, while he didn't know specifically that they had planned a bachelor auction to raise money to rebuild Southlake Park where he'd grown up, he knew that they were attempting to make changes to the neighborhood. Aside from keeping up with Kadaris, he also followed the local newspaper online, so he knew efforts were being made to revitalize the neighborhood which is what led him to the long thought out decision he'd finally made.

Growing up around Peaches Brighton aka Mama Peaches, you had no choice but to appreciate and savor good cooking. But being her son, Jeremy was constantly around it, to the point it made him want to become a cook, one who could serve up the most mouthwatering dishes across the varying kinds of cuisine.

By the time he graduated from high school, he had been accepted to San Diego Culinary Institute as well as the University of San Diego for which he planned to major in business administration and minor in entrepreneurship. It was a great task ahead of him, but he finished culinary school at the top of his class and graduated magna cum laude.

His ultimate goal was to own his own restaurant, maybe even a chain of them. He just didn't want to do it in Chicago. He wanted to do it where no one knew Mama Peaches and how she threw down in the kitchen. He didn't want anyone comparing his dishes to hers.

Two failed attempts at opening restaurants only to

have them close within the first year threatened his push to manifest his dream. And it wasn't because he wasn't a good cook, but rather he was trying to open the restaurants in locations that didn't desire his type of cuisine. He just could never get enough foot traffic.

Even though his mom wasn't privy to his heavy heart concerning his restaurant failures when he was last home to visit her, he heavily weighed giving up heart's desire and settle for continuing to work as head chef at the current restaurant he was at in San Diego. At least he'd still be doing what he loved, cooking.

However, rummaging through some of his dad's old things, he found a letter he had written to congratulate him on the opening of the first restaurant. Problem was, he never received the letter from his father because he passed weeks before it opened. Reading his father's praise of him going after his dream and achieving it reignited his passion to prosper with his restaurant.

But this time around, he knew if he was going to succeed with his plan, Chicago really was the market for him. After much research, query, and that constant nagging in his gut, he had finally accepted a reality he had been denying for years. Even though the city already had scores of restaurants for the millions of people crowding the city, he knew people were always eager to try out new spots. He was counting on him creating the right atmosphere and bomb cuisine to garner him tons of repeat patrons and adulation in his hometown.

His mom didn't know about his plans, but once he returned to Chicago, all his time would be spent on opening his restaurant in Southlake Park. If their plans to rehab it came to fruition, he'd be more than able to afford a storefront space there for his dream restaurant.

One may think that after hearing his mother say the bachelor auction is what was needed to fund the final cost to complete their plans, he would readily agree to be a bachelor, but that wasn't his style.

He was a determined man, just not a by any means necessary kind of man. With that resolve, he'd figure out a way to help them get the funds to bring the neighborhood back from the dead, he just wouldn't exploit his looks to do so.

He laughed at the absurdity of it all as he packed his marinara sauce to store in the refrigerator before he got ready to head into work.

While he wasn't able to be the top chef and owner of his own restaurant, cooking was so much a part of his DNA that he settled for being the top chef in someone else's kitchen. The five star restaurant he currently worked at sated his cooking appetite until his next move.

He smiled as he locked his apartment door knowing he'd see his dream come true. He had every intention of succeeding this next go round.

2

Friendships are interesting. Some last a lifetime and then others are just a for a season. But in the mix of that, there are friends who can not speak to one another for days, weeks, months, and even years but pick right up with one another as if no time elapsed between them. The latter is what Naima was eventually counting on as she stared at her phone.

The right corner of her mouth inched higher as she finally forced herself to click on his name.

Life back at home for her had become so torturous after her divorce and tumultuous events at her last job that kept her away from social media, but now that she had completely severed ties from her ex-husband, she had more time to herself. More time to explore who she was and what she wanted. And the guy filling her screen was definitely someone she wanted.

"Good Lord!" she gasped but then covered her mouth as she looked around the living room, making sure she hadn't alerted her grandmother, Geraldine Jenkins.

It had been two weeks since she'd left Norfolk, Virginia and moved to Chicago to live with her grandmother and be around her best friend, her cousin, Khloe Madison who lived in the apartment above them. The move was her fresh start.

Jeremy had always been attractive to her which is why she was grateful that her grandmother was best friends with his mother, Peaches Brighton, better known as Mama Peaches.

The closeness of the ladies meant that when she was younger, she was freely able to spend all her time during her summers in Chicago at his house and around him. Pining after him. It was a pity that he never noticed how much she liked him. Like a lost puppy looking for its home, she used to camp out in the kitchen with him while he worked on perfecting varying recipes and dishes.

From all the sampling he did from his own food and the fact that Mama Peaches was an amazing cook, it stood to reason why Jeremy was quite chubby back then, but still very much cute to her. In her eyes, he was her first crush, her first love. The man whose Facebook profile she currently stared at looked drastically different from the chubby one she adored back then.

She shifted on the couch as she stared at the picture of him. The man had the nerve to have nothing on but an apron and a pair of jogging pants while hoisting up a pasta and chicken dish in front of him as he posed for the camera. As if the human eye could even focus on the food on the plate when *he* was the one holding it.

He was spectacular. *When did he get all of those tattoos? And the muscles underneath them?* She couldn't help but to bite her bottom lip and pull it into her mouth as she did a thorough scan of him.

The man looked like a lean pro football player.

With how tight the apron was tied around his waist, she could see it was trim versus the way his upper body sprouted out like a sculpted triangle he obviously crafted from rigorous workouts.

And that smile of his. It was something she always loved about him. It was so bright and endearing. And when her eyes focused in on his, her breathing pattern shifted. They weren't mischievous like a man of his physique and good looks might show, they were just warm and engaging.

His hair was cut low with deep waves and his full, long glossy beard outlined full but soft looking lips she'd always wanted to kiss growing up, but he never took the bait she subtly threw his way.

"So you're just going to keep ogling him like that? And out in the open? Sure you don't want to go get tucked in your room and continue perusing his pictures?" Khloe lifted a perfectly arched eyebrow at her favorite cousin.

Naima's eyes bulged wider as she flipped her phone over. "Oh, shut up Khloe." Naima snipped before she covered her face with both of her hands in shame.

Khloe laughed as she flopped down on the couch across from Naima.

Naima peeked through her hands to glimpse at her cousin. "How long were you standing behind me?"

"Long enough to see that you still have a crush on him. I mean, I don't blame you, he is fine." She opened the bottled water in her hand and took a swig of it.

"I don't-"

"Really, Naima?" With a slight grin on her face, Khloe cocked her head at her cousin.

"Okay, so yes I had a crush on him when we were younger. And yes, he is fine now, if that's how he still looks." She mumbled the last of her words. "How often does he come back to Chicago?" She sat up with a glimmer of hope and wonder in her voice.

Khloe's wide smile returned to her face. "Not often. But let's discuss the fact that you are a beautiful, free woman," she cocked her head at Naima, "who can be attracted to whatever man she wants to. And if that man so happens to be Jeremy, that's perfectly fine."

"Why'd you say free like that?" Naima closed her laptop before placing it on the coffee table in front of her.

"Oh, you came to town acting brand new I see. Not throwing it in your face, but you're free from that ex-husband of yours."

"Oh, him." Naima picked up a throw pillow from the couch and pulled it close to her chest as she tucked her legs under her.

Khloe settled more into the couch as she waited for her cousin to give the cue if she wanted to continue to talk about him or switch the subject altogether.

"You know, I thought he was the one and that we would have the perfect life together." Naima finally looked up at Khloe.

"But he wasn't and it's good you found that out as early into your marriage as you did and not decades later."

"But I should've seen the signs before we even got

married. You know, I was a corporate event coordinator and I met him working on an account. He swept me off my feet with his charm." A small smile stretched her face. A bit of nostalgia settled in her eyes as they focused on Khloe, but she soon shook the look away with the rattling of her head. "I can't believe we got married in such a short time. Too short of a time."

"Yeah, Nana went on about that for months," Khloe chimed in.

"I know." Naima let out a soft chuckle. "Even with her sordid past of men, she wasted no time in telling me that I hadn't taken the proper amount of time to get to learn him."

"Well, with her past with men, Nana is worth listening to at times."

"I know, but I didn't see that at the time. I was a fool in love and paid no mind to how controlling he was. I thought it was romantic and caring for him to be so into and concerned about every detail of my life. I thought he was the answer to my prayers. But it turns out he wasn't. We weren't a good fit." Her eyes darted away from her cousin's. She still hadn't shared what else her ex-husband had done, but she wanted to leave it and him in the past, so she wouldn't share it now either.

"You darn right you two weren't." Geraldine said, walking into the living room, wiping her hands on a dish towel.

Khloe shot Naima an apologetic look, knowing the rant that would ensue. Hoping to take the attention off Naima and redirect Geraldine's attention, Khloe perked up and said, "Nana, how are you?"

"I'm good and I know what you're doing."

Geraldine eyed her granddaughter.

"What, just showering my love on you." Khloe stood, walked over to Geraldine and wrapped her arms around her.

"Yeah, yeah, yeah. That ain't all you're doing. You're trying to take my attention off Naima and that good for nothing ex of hers."

"Nana, not today. Please?" Khloe begged as she held on to her.

"Not today? If she wouldn't have married him that day she did, I wouldn't be here today," she pointed towards the ground "talking about how gritty he was, is."

Naima got up from the couch and wrapped her arms around her grandmother on the side opposite of Khloe.

The two little chocolate beauties squeezed their fairly taller grandmother tighter as Naima spoke up and said, "Aw, Nana, we just love you so much."

Khloe chuckled as she tapped Naima on her arm, signaling her to squeeze Geraldine tighter.

"I love you both too, but get off of me. You're squeezing me so tight, you might make my wig pop off my head."

With riotous laughter, Naima clutched her chest and Khloe held her side. The ladies soon stepped back from their grandmother.

"Oh, Nana, we have to get you to the store and get you a better wig then," Naima said as she rejoined her seat on the couch.

Out of her grandmother's sight, Khloe shook her head and put her pointer finger up to her mouth, egging Naima to hush.

Geraldine put her hand on her hip and cocked her head to the side as she stared at Naima. "Did Peaches put you up to that?"

"Hunh, Nana?" Naima's tone was uncertain as her eyebrows squished together, staring at Geraldine.

"Trying to get me to get a new wig?" Her eyes narrowed in on Naima as she pointed a stiff finger at her. "I'mma tell you just like I tell her all the time, ain't nothing wrong with the collection of wigs I have. But there's something wrong with your man-coding skills. If you're here for good like you say you are, you best believe, I ain't letting you tie another knot make sure both ends of the string are sturdy."

"Nana, I know I was stupid for being with him as long as I was." Naima groaned and pouted.

Geraldine sighed as she let herself down on the couch next to Naima. She grabbed her hand and squeezed it. "You're not stupid, baby. We've all been there before." Geraldine ran her tongue across her teeth as she briefly looked away from her granddaughter.

"I know, Nana, I just can't believe I played myself like a fool with him."

"But you woke up from it, Naima," Khloe chimed in.

"Yeah, but I didn't get out without a fight. Because he wanted to keep up appearances, he fought me tooth and nail before he finally agreed to give me a divorce, even when he was the cause of it." She mumbled the last of her words and her body tensed recounting the things he'd done during the course of their marriage.

"But that bastard finally gave it to you and that's what matters. You're here with us now." Geraldine looked over at Khloe before looking back at Naima. "You may not have been able to stay at that company you loved working for, but you're in Chi-town now where I'm certain plenty of firms will be willing to hire my sweet pea." She patted Naima's hand again. "Plus, I'll be able to keep my eye on who you end up with next."

Naima's eyes darted towards Khloe's. She wished she could telepathically tell her cousin that she hoped that her grandmother wouldn't meddle in her love life or lack thereof. More importantly, she hoped her Nana would never become privy to her apparent resurrected crush on Jeremy.

3

Jeremy's large fist hung in mid-air ready to knock on his mother's door when he remembered there was no need to do so. He chuckled at himself as he reached into his pocket and grabbed his keys and inserted the one with the red rubber ring around it into the lock chamber, twisting it to the left.

He had seen his dad's Cadillac parked in front of the house, so he knew she was at home. That was a good thing, because otherwise, her not being there would ruin his surprise.

He hung his coat in the small closet at the front door and then made his way through the living room that opened into the dining room. He knew not to step into either of the bedrooms just off the dining room to search for her whereabouts since he heard several voices coming from the kitchen at the back of the two flat his parents had converted into a single-family home well before he was born.

One of the voices he knew was his mother's and after an accusatory "Peaches" rang out in the kitchen, he knew it had to be no one other than Ms. Geraldine. But the third voice, he was unfamiliar with. Had his mother taken in another foster child? A girl at that?

Growing up, she'd only ever fostered boys, but maybe now that she'd gotten older, she wanted feminine energy around her.

His steps sped up wanting to see if the sweet voice that seemed to hold his mother and Geraldine's attention was indeed a teenager. She didn't sound like it. Her voice had more seasoning, life to it than that of a young girl, but if it were a young girl, he'd demand that he speak to his mother alone immediately.

Just last year, he told her that at her age, he didn't think it was safe for her to have foster kids in the house anymore, no matter how spry of a woman she claimed to be. He was certain she couldn't get around and upside a boy's head if need be the way she could when she was younger.

While Kadaris checked in on her often, neither of them was with her 24/7. He'd hate if something happened to his mother at the hands of one of these new age fools up in her house giving her hell.

He went to the house to surprise his mother, but it was him who was truly surprised when he crossed the threshold of the kitchen and he looked up to see that the sweet voice he couldn't identify belonged to Naima Grant.

"Naima?" His voice pitched higher as he stared at her with her hair in twists down to her butt and that cocoa cinnamon skin of hers glowing against the canary yellow sweater she wore.

Naima's mouth fell open slightly as she took in

Jeremy standing in front of her. Although he was fine, appetizing in each of them, his Facebook pictures did not do him the justice owed to him.

She found herself crossing her legs tighter at the apex of her thighs the longer she stared at him.

Those mesmerizing, medium brown, smizing eyes of his and the way his soft looking and long beard framed those full, pink lips of his. The man had toasted almond skin and perfect, pink lips. His lips weren't moving, but they called out to her.

She brushed her hand along her mouth, unsure of if she had actually drooled staring at him.

"Naima, what are you waiting on? Get up and give the man a hug," Geraldine said, clearly cutting into her thoughts as she watched her blinking granddaughter stare at Jeremy not too far from her with his hands outstretched.

"Come here girl." He chuckled as he pulled her much shorter frame into him and gave her a bear hug.

She took a deep inhale, reveling in the citrus clean scent that weakened her knees and made her want him to pull her in even closer. Fuse their bodies together for as long as possible and give her unlimited access to his embrace.

His rigid muscles pressing into her made her eyes flutter closed. Everything about him was sexy. His looks, his smell and that gruff voice of his as he spoke wrapped themselves around her and put her in the daze she was currently in as he gently pushed her back an arm's length to get a good look at her.

"Wow, I haven't seen you in years. You look great. How are you?" His naturally tight, bright eyes observed her.

"You loo-look-"

Geraldine shook her head. "Naima, make that cat loose your tongue and speak up. As tight as y'all were when you were younger, I thought you'd be more happy to see him. Come here boy." Geraldine motioned for Jeremy to come towards her, but Peaches' voice altered his footsteps' direction.

Jeremy squeezed Naima's shoulders before he walked away from her.

"You better not go hug her before you hug me. What are you doing here anyway?" Mama Peaches stood from the table and propped her hands on her hips.

"Aww, momma, you know I love you. I was saving the best hug for last."

Naima watched the muscles flex and bulge on his back as Jeremy engulfed his mother in his embrace and lifted her off the ground.

She took the moment with his back turned to her to close her mouth since she was still in shock with how beautiful he was in person and then to smooth out her eyebrows, straighten out her clothes, and make sure her twists were kempt. His presence had thrown her for an unexpected loop. Had her insides all topsy turvy.

"Boy, put me down." Mama Peaches wiggled in his arms as Jeremy gently placed her back down on her feet.

When he let her go, she popped him on his arm before she pulled him back into her for another hug and kissed his cheek. She pulled away from him again and with a thick voice said, "You know I'm always happy to see you son, but why are you here and better yet, why didn't you tell me you were coming? I would've prepared something for you." She angled her head to look up at him.

Naima eagerly awaited his answer. Since she was in Chicago, she was hoping that he would somehow find his way there too. She wanted to see him and there he was, all six plus feet inches of Sir Fineness in the flesh.

Traveling her thoughts, her face scrunched up. *Why hadn't he told Mama Peaches he was coming home?* Had she known he'd be there that night, she would've put even more thought into her outfit. It was cute, but the oversized and cropped sweater, dark skinny jeans, and brown combat boots were worn more so for comfort and warmth, given she was only over to discuss the bachelor auction fast approaching with the older ladies.

If she would've known he was coming, she wouldn't have hesitated to wear a more form-fitting top and her brown wedges that she knew made her butt look even more round than the ample one she was blessed with.

She shook her head at her musings. The man hadn't even been in the room a good five minutes and he had consumed her every thought, but thinking on the brotherly way he hugged her and how he never seemed to notice her like that, she reasoned she was probably the least of his concerns. Her shoulders slumped and she sighed as she walked the short distance back to her seat.

"Me being here wouldn't have been a surprise if I would've told you about it now, would it?" He winked and then pulled her into him again.

"Boy, you know I don't like surprises," she said, wrestling herself away from him. "Have a seat." She motioned for him to take the seat next to her.

"I will, just let me give Ms. Geraldine a hug."

"That's right baby, you never forget about me." Geraldine stood up and accepted Jeremy's hug and kissed his cheek before she rejoined her seat.

"Okay, pleasantries are all out of the way. So now really tell me what brought you here and how long you'll be here." Mama Peaches aimed her words at her son.

With a grin on his face, Jeremy shook his head as he stared at his mother. "I-"

"You know what I know, you better not be showing up here today as an excuse for you not coming back for the bachelor auction a couple of weeks away because you know I need you in it."

Naima sat up straight hearing the last of Mama Peaches words. *If Jeremy will be a bachelor, maybe I'll bid on him.*

"Ma, pretty little lady," he reached for her hand, "we talked about this. I will not be a bachelor in the auction."

Mama Peaches' lips curled up in displeasure as she snatched her hand from his.

He gripped it again and pulled it up to his lips to kiss the back of her hand.

Naima studied him. That's all she could manage to do since he entered the room. The man was just that fine. She didn't get the chance to linger on her thoughts before he spoke again.

"But, I can at least help y'all out with it in some way."

"I told you I wasn't looking for money from you boys, I was looking for y'all to pay it forward with your time and services. And you're saying you'll come back so soon for the special day?"

He smiled wide, exposing those perfect white teeth of his.

Naima sat quiet and still, not wanting to miss any of what was being said. Jeremy seemed intent on not being a bachelor in the auction, but how long was he in town this time? And would him coming back again so soon give him and her time to catch up? Explore her renewed interest in him?

"Ma, I don't have to come back in town because I'm not leaving it again."

"Hunh?" The question fumbled out of Mama Peaches' mouth

He chuckled looking at her flinching back and her eyebrows squishing together.

"I moved back to Chicago. Surprise." He smiled and his arms stretched wide as if he were presenting himself to her as a gift.

"Jeremy, don't lie to me." Mama Peaches' voice elevated.

"I'm not, Ma. I'm back here to stay. Actually, I bought a two flat three blocks over."

Her neck snapped at him. "You mean to tell me you bought a house here, in Southlake Park, and didn't tell me that either?" Overwhelmed with joy and shock that her son was moving back home and would be so close to her, and equally annoyed that he hadn't told her about it, she wiped the tears from her face with one hand and popped him on his arm with the other.

He laughed as he leaned forward and rubbed her back. "Lady, I wanted this to be a surprise for you. You're always on me about moving back home and starting a family here. I thought you'd be happy about this."

With her dark brown eyes wide and her mouth gaped open, Mama Peaches practically jumped in her seat as she rotated to fully face him. "So I get a daughter-in-law and a grandbaby out of this move too?"

Naima sat up straight. From her perusal of his Facebook page, none of his posts or photos screamed or whispered that he was in a relationship, let alone that he had a woman pregnant. Her ears burned as she awaited his response.

She was ready to listen to his response, but she also studied his body language. Him sighing and shaking his head as he looked over at his frantic mother offered her a glimmer of hope that Mama Peaches was jumping the gun with her assumptions and she might have a chance with him after all.

"Jeremy, I can't believe you hadn't told me that you're in a serious relationship."

"Ma-"

"Why have you been hiding her from me?"

"Ma-"

"Is it because she's pregnant and you thought I would get on you about the baby in the carriage before marriage?"

"Ma, there is no she and there is no baby on the way. I'm just as single today as I was the last time I talked to you."

Naima released a soft breath she wasn't even aware she was holding.

"I'll tell you later on exactly why I moved back, but for now, can we all just enjoy the fact that I'm back home?" He smiled that flawless smile of his at her.

The corners of Naima's mouth lifted at the mention of him being back in Chicago like she was. It wasn't her childhood home, but her vacations from school spent there made it feel more like home for her than Norfolk ever did. And for the life of her, she couldn't understand from where and why the resurgence of her crush on Jeremy had come from. But it was a welcomed one.

Still misty-eyed, Mama Peaches stared at Jeremy before she cupped his face with both hands and pulled him into her to place a kiss on his forehead. "Welcome home, baby."

"I love you too, ma."

"I love you more," she said as she pulled back to look at him. "Okay, even though I ain't getting a grandbaby just yet," she pointed a stiff finger and darted a stern squint his way, "you moving back finally, is cause to celebrate." With a big smile on her face, she clapped her hands first and said, "So who's cooking the celebration dinner, me or you?

His head reared back as one of those naturally sharp eyebrows of his lifted. "Me cook? No ma'am, since you're the better cook, I think you should." He winked at her.

"Boy, with what I taught you, your own experience, plus your degree skills, you better get up and get to work." Pushing his elbow, she nudged him out of his seat. "Gon' and whip us up your welcome home dinner. It'd be a beautiful sight to see such a handsome man like yourself cooking for three lovely ladies like us." She smirked.

"Y'all not gon' tell her to cook for me since I'm the

one that just came home?" Jeremy eyed Geraldine and Naima.

"Nope. Not at all. You know I love your cooking and I'm just glad I wore my eating pants today." Geraldine chuckled as she adjusted in her seat.

Naima merely smirked as she rested her face in her hands propped up by the table.

"You're not gonna come to my defense, Naima? You always used to." He feigned a pout.

His semi puckered lips made Naima shift in her seat as he kept his gaze on her. She cleared her throat before a hushed "Nope" escaped her lips.

"Man, what kind of welcome home is this?" He shook his head as he stood from the table and walked to the stainless-steel refrigerator he ordered when he had her kitchen renovated some years back. He pulled one of the doors and looked in it. "You should be catering to me, not the other way around." He chuckled as he pulled at items on the shelves.

"What are you looking for, boy?" Mama Peaches asked.

Deep in thought, he didn't respond, but instead shuffled over to the cabinets, pulled them all open and stepped back with his hands on his hips as he scanned the shelves.

"Jeremy, what is it you're looking for? Because if Peaches doesn't have it, maybe I do," Geraldine asked, just as curious as Peaches obviously was given the way her arm perched on the back of her chair and her mouth flattened as she stared at her son.

He turned around and sighed, looking at them. "Thanks, Ms. Geraldine, but I'm certain if my momma doesn't have it, you don't either. Well ma, I guess you'll just have to cook what you were gonna cook for dinner." He grinned as he headed back to his seat, but her booming voice stopped in him in his tracks.

"No sir, you know where the grocery store is around here. Gon' head and run up there and get what you need so you can get back here and get to cooking and making this place smell good. Shoot, got my stomach growling just thinking about how good it's gonna taste." Mama Peaches held a wicked smile on her face as she began reorganizing the papers on the table.

Jeremy just stared at her.

Geraldine fell in line with Mama Peach's persistence not to cook and grabbed a paper to read.

Naima merely stared at him as he gawked at his mother incredulously.

"Gon' Jeremy," Mama Peaches' voice was more stern than it was before.

"Alright ladies, I'll be back." He headed towards the opening of the kitchen.

"And why are you still sitting there? Get up and go with him," Geraldine ordered Naima as she stared at her.

"Hunh, Nana?" Naima wasn't exactly sure she understood why her grandmother gave her the command.

"You heard her, Naima. Go to the store with him. It ain't like y'all don't know each other. Besides, with the plans you know and helped to reorganize for the bachelor auction, maybe you can convince him to actually be one."

Jeremy swiftly turned and mouthed to Naima, "Not going to happen."

She chuckled as she stood from her seat and

immediately began moving her twists around and smoothing out her clothes since Jeremy still had his eyes her.

Okay you two, don't come up with any more ideas for that night while I'm gone. Just wait until I get back so that I can keep y'all in line with what's on budget and what's realistic. There will be no men riding into the cultural center on horses.

"Oh, hush girl and get out of here with him," Geraldine said over her shoulder.

"Well, I'll be back ladies." She grabbed her purse and walked up to Jeremy. "You ready to go?" She strained her neck looking up at him.

"Yup, Ima."

She blushed as her words slowly left her mouth. "I didn't think you would even remember calling me that."

"Now Ima, you were one of my homies back in the day. How could I forget you your nickname or you for that matter?"

She gave him a half grin at the mention of him referring to her as one of his homies back then. To her back then, there was nothing homie about him and taking in that clean smell of his, the beautiful dark brown eyes staring down at her, and the sexy smile he obviously didn't know how potent it was, homie wasn't how she viewed him at that point either.

When she didn't say anything else, he pulled her under his arm as they walked down the hallway. "We can use this time to play catch up with each other."

"Okay." Her words came out weak, again hating the way he referred to her as his homie and the way he held her to his side, almost in a headlock, like a homie. She wanted to be so much more with him.

4

"Thanks for warming up your car before we got in it." Naima shimmied in the heated leather seat. "Coming here for Christmas breaks was not enough time to get my body used to this weather." She rubbed her hands together seeing as though they were still cold.

"Shoot, growing up in it doesn't make you comfortable with it either. We just deal with it."

"True."

He chuckled as he squeezed her knee. "So what has little Ima been up to all these years and how long are you here for?" Jeremy turned a corner.

Naima didn't readily respond. She wasn't sure if it was the heat from the seat under her, or the heat from his strong hand gripping her knee that had her insides ablaze. She did and she didn't want him to move his hand. Perhaps inch it up her thigh?

Ever since she'd seen him walk into the kitchen, every little movement he made, every sound he made scintillated her.

Thinking it was best that she get his hand off her,

31

she cleared her throat as she shifted in her seat and said, "Nothing, just adulting. I've been living out my dream, coordinating events on the corporate level and enjoying my life as best as I can. That's all." She folded her arms across her chest, grazing her hardened nipples, which in turn caused her to squeeze the peak of her thighs even closer together. The distinctive smell of his inebriating cologne and what had to be mixed with his natural scent in the confines of the car and just being in his presence was a lot for her to digest.

"Seems like you left something out?" He chuckled.

"Hunh?" She stared at his side profile as he parked the car in front of Southlake Park Market.

He took his foot off the brake and looked at her. "You forgot to mention that you've also been busy being a wife."

Her eyes widened at him knowing she'd been married.

He grinned. "It should be no surprise that with who my mother is and who your grandmother is that I wouldn't know that you're married. Is he here too? Joining you soon?"

"Was married," Naima said barely above a whisper as she grabbed her purse and opened her car door.

He jumped out and ran around to her side of the car. "Hey, I was going to get that for you." Holding onto the passenger side door, he stepped back and let her pass him by. "Hey," he pulled on her shoulder, forcing her to halt her rapid footsteps towards the entrance of the store, "did I say something wrong?" His forehead wrinkled as he stared down at her.

She looked up at him, but then pursed her lips

before she shifted her eyes to a spot past him. "No. I just don't want to talk about him."

"Sorry."

She turned to walk away, but he pulled on her arm, thwarting her departure yet again. "Hey, I know we didn't do a good job of keeping up with one another over the years, but I'd like to think the summers and winter breaks we spent in my kitchen together, talking and laughing nonstop were enough to let you know that you can talk to me about anything if need be. No judgment. No matter how much time has passed with us not talking."

Her close to black, oval eyes lined with black mascara, making her bright eyes pop even more looked up into his. "Yeah, I know I can." She whispered unsure if her voice would shake having to briefly relive thoughts of her husband mixed in with her growing desire for Jeremy. There was just something about him, his presence that captivated her. Spoke of his sincerity and compassion. Those qualities alone and seeing that he still possessed them were enough to draw her back to him like a magnet.

In a world full of men bent on proving their masculinity with how many women they could bed have no regard for the women, she could already see that Jeremy hadn't fallen into that kind of toxic masculinity. That was refreshing.

"Good. So we don't have to talk about him if you don't want to, but if you do, I'm here for you. Now let's go in here and get what I need to get my momma off my back for the night."

Naima laughed. "Yeah, just off your back about

cooking dinner for her, because I'm certain she's not going to let up on you being a bachelor in the auction." She stepped through the door he held open for her. Once a few feet inside the store, she turned to look back at him. "What's up with you not wanting to be one?" *I'm certain they'd raise a lot of money off you.* She was grateful that her misguided thoughts hadn't slipped out of her mouth, but the bright light in the store made her more aware of just how handsome he was than the lights in Mama Peaches' kitchen.

"Come on now, Naima, you gon' act like you don't remember how much of a loner I am?" He side-eyed her.

His facial expression made her smile. "No, I remember that, I just thought you had grown out of the boy you were back then."

"Don't get it twisted, I'm a man now, but still a loner. I have no desire to be like prime rib on a cutting board in front of those women. That's just not my style."

"Okay, gotcha." She held her hands up as if in defeat as she flashed a smile at him.

"Good," he said as she chuckled and pulled her into a headlock under his left arm.

"Jeremy," she screamed as she broke free from his hold.

"What?" he asked her, laughing. "I used to put you in a headlock all the time back in the day."

"Well, this ain't back in the day." She instantly regretted the snip in her voice. There she was, silently fawning over him and he was manhandling her like she was a boy. She wasn't a boy. She was all woman. All five foot two inches of her and she wished that he could see her, her femininity, her desire to be more than friends. Just like she wished back when they were younger.

"My bad. I won't put you in a headlock anymore. Here, let me make sure they're straight." He gripped her arms, making her face him and to stop pulling on her twists. He grabbed the three shadowing the front of her face and flipped them to the back of her head. "There, perfect just like you were before."

Him calling her perfect made her wonder if perhaps she was reading him wrong. Maybe he was feeling her and just hadn't said anything about it. But when a taller woman walked by and winked at Jeremy and his eyes followed her until they landed on the woman's backside while she clearly overexaggerated her gait, Naima's hope that Jeremy was into her dissipated. "Typical male," she mumbled under her breath as she pulled her purse closer to her.

"What did you say?" Jeremy asked barely turning to face her as he continued to watch the woman who was looking back at him with a noticeable longing in her eyes.

"Jeremy, you want to tell me what to go get while you hook up with your little friend over there?"

"What?" His face scrunched up as he looked back at her. Not sure of what she had said and seeing that her tight lips didn't seem interested in opening to repeat herself he said, "Come on, let's get a cart and get what I need."

He brushed past her, pulled a cart towards him and then guided it towards the meat section of the store. "I see this place hasn't changed." He looked down the aisles he passed. "So, you never said how long you were visiting."

"I didn't say I was visiting." She grumbled. She knew she was doing a poor job of masking her attitude, but she just couldn't help herself. Liking Jeremy had always been her thing. She would've thought a few boyfriends and even a husband later would have rid her of her juvenile crush, but clearly her feelings hadn't got that memo. He had a calm to him that a woman could just lose herself in a man like him.

The shift in her attitude wasn't lost on him. His eyes darted towards her. "What's up? What's wrong with you?"

"Nothing. I'm straight. So, what are you cooking?" She barely looked at him.

"Nah, you answer my question first and then I'll answer yours." He grinned.

She was quiet as she walked aside him. A few paces later, she no longer felt him next to her. She looked back and frowned at him.

His high-arching eyebrows raised higher.

"Okay. Okay." She sighed, slightly stomping towards him. "I'm not visiting, I moved here."

"Really?"

She nodded and couldn't help but smile given the elated expression on his face.

"Cool, Naima. It makes my homecoming even better. If you remember, I wasn't cool with anyone back then but you, Kadaris, and Khloe."

She shifted on one leg as she looked up at him. "You know, I never understood that. With as many boys that Mama Peaches fostered in your house, I was sure that you would've been more outgoing and had a lot more friends, brothers. Quite a few of them stayed around a great deal of time."

"I think that's why I was a loner, because there were so many people in my house. And don't get me wrong, I don't resent my mother for being the way she was. With her taking in foster kids all of the time, I knew I had to share her and her love. Real talk, those kids needed her more than me. She was definitely there for me, but because I also had my pops, I accepted their love and learned to keep to myself. Outside of you three, I was comfortable with my solitude."

His solitude was another thing that drew her to him. She had seen the varying kinds of boys in and out of the house, from those labeled juvenile delinquents on up to mute ones and yet Jeremy had maintained his chill and nerdy demeanor. He never felt the need to follow the flow of the others. Their conversation was steadily strengthening her interest in him. "I mean, I can understand that." She bit her lip out of nervousness at the odd way he was looking at her. She nudged the cart with her right hand, forcing him to grip the handle and set it back in motion. Her mood lightened as she fell in stride alongside him. "Okay, so I answered your question, now answer mine. What are we eating for dinner?"

He stopped and flashed that insanely gorgeous smile of his. "Oh, so 'we' eating?" He wagged his hand between the two of them. "You staying for some of my cooking? Admit it, you miss it?"

She covered her mouth to quell her laughter, but he tugged on her arm. "Naw, naw. Let me hear and see you say it, because I distinctly remember you clowning my cooking back in the day, yet you never left anything on your plate. But now, now you're asking what I'm cooking as if you plan to smash it the minute it's done."

"Whatever." She turned her face away, knowing her smile was wider than her small face probably allowed. Her cheeks started to hurt. She looked back at him, pursing her lips to lessen her smile. "So, I may be just a little hungry." She held her pinched fingers in the air as she squinted at him.

His smile grew wider, sexier, as if that were even possible.

"But, but," she held up her hand to calm his ego, "in my defense, I was seated all day right where you saw me with them mapping out the flow of the bachelor auction. Those two are so demanding." She shook her head, recalling her day with the older ladies.

"That should be nothing new to you." He chuckled as he set them back in motion.

"Well, little Ms. Rumbling Gut, I'll be making pan-seared chicken breasts and sweet potato noodles with almond sauce. And for the drink, I think, if they have it, we'll have Pinot Noir."

Even at a young age, his confident way around the kitchen was honestly always that added umph that made her so attracted to him. It was the je ne sais quoi on top of his calm, but humorous spirit.

Him knowing what he wanted to do life long back then was admirable.

Their time at the grocery store had quickly revealed to her why her attraction to him was so strong.

She wanted to be with him because he was still proving to be a great catch like she'd always viewed him.

He was attentive. Even the assurance in his eyes and words when he said she could talk to him about anything spoke to her soul even though she didn't mouth the confidence in him to him. That comfort he sought to provide her was like a welcome salve compared to the wounds her ex inflicted on her.

She was confident that she didn't want to use Jeremy's desired affections towards her to help her get past her ex. She was over that loser, but rather she had always been attracted to him, but distance and time hadn't been on their side back then. But now that it seemed to line them up together, she wanted to capitalize on the favor and see just what could transpire between them.

If ever he only felt what she felt for him, they could work.

When he realized she wasn't still walking beside him, he stopped and looked back at her. "What, you don't drink wine? You don't have to have any if you don't want to. No pressure."

She remained silent.

"Wait, are you doubting my skills to pull that dish off?" That sexy eyebrow of his peaked again.

"No." She shook her head, shaking herself out of her reverie. Not willing or ready to share what she was really thinking, she kept the conversation focused on food. "You didn't even list the ingredients, but it just sounded so good that it really did make my stomach rumble. I'm really hungry." She walked up to him. "How long will it take you to make all of that?"

He grinned. "Not long. I can do it with my eyes closed."

"I bet." She pulled her bottom lip into her mouth thinking of what else he could *do.*

"Naima, you straight?" Jeremy asked, trying to regain her attention.

"Uh, yeah." She started walking again. "So, what made you come back after all of these years?" she asked as they stopped in front of the butcher's deli case.

"Hold on, Naima." He looked at her before directing his attention to the butcher. "Can I get six of those chicken breasts?" He tapped on the case in front of him.

She stood near, poking at a loaf of wheat, sandwich bread.

She noticed his countenance change as he turned to look at her. That avoiding look he had when his mother asked why he returned reappeared as he eyed her.

He stuffed his hands into his jean pockets. He stared at her longer before he lifted one hand to his face and rubbed it over before it settled on his beard as he pulled on the lengthy, full hairs on his chin. "I won't say just yet, but it was more so out of necessity. A recent realization I'm still coming to terms with." He angled his body slightly away from her.

"Hey," she pulled on his arm, forcing him to look back at her, "just like you told me earlier that I can talk to you," she squeezed his arm, "you know you can talk to me-"

"Chicken breasts?" The butcher called from over the counter.

Jeremy grabbed the meat from the man and turned to face Naima and dropped the meat into the cart.

"Jeremy, you know you can talk to me, right?" She stepped closer to him.

"Yeah," his eyes were dull for a brief second before his face lit up with that effervescent smile of his. "Let's just get the rest of the ingredients so we can feed you girl." He pulled on her hand, placing it on the cart's handle as if he needed her help in steering the cart.

Naima let it go for the moment, but she had no intention of letting up on him opening up to her. She wanted to be there for him as much as he said he would be there for her.

5

"Jeremy, you sure did put your foot and toes up in this chicken and noodles. What kind are they again?" Geraldine asked, stuffing her mouth with another forkful of food.

"Thanks, Ms. Geraldine. They're sweet potato noodles. I love to cook traditional meals, but I also love to put more healthy spins on the foods we love so much. Everyone loves pasta and pasta dishes, so if I can create them not using pasta and make them taste good, then I'm always down for that." He twirled his fork in the noodles and then braced his spoon at the end of the fork to keep the noodles from dangling off.

Trying not to be obvious and yet enjoying every morsel of her food, Naima constantly stole glances of Jeremy.

Mama Peaches shook her head. "Lord, I wonder what my Harold would say if he saw his grown son eating noodles with a fork *and* a spoon. He'd probably say we failed you."

"Peaches, leave that boy alone. You know he has to

put that cooking degree of his to use." Geraldine sipped some of her water and then looked over at her granddaughter. "And what's wrong with you? Why are you so quiet?"

"Look at her plate. It's empty. She didn't have time to talk when she was too busy stuffing her face." Jeremy laughed as he stood from his chair and reached across the table to grab Naima's plate. "Here, let me put you some more chicken and noodles on there since you were so hungry at the store. Clearly, you enjoyed what I cooked."

Your cooking is not the only thing I want to enjoy. "No, Jeremy. While it was good, I couldn't possibly eat anymore."

He eyed her for a bit and from the angle standing up afforded him, he could see her food belly. "You're right. Anymore to eat and those tight pants of yours are going to pop."

"Oh, shut up." She grinned as she threw a napkin at him.

He remained standing, laughing at her.

She shook her head at him, before covering her face in shame.

"Leave that girl alone. Since you want to serve seconds, add some more of that chicken to my plate." Mama Peaches handed him her plate and watched him walk to the stove top to heed her request. "Lord knows I'm glad that you're back here for good, that means I have a personal chef now."

He snapped his neck at her.

She bucked her head at him. "You heard me, a personal chef." Her shoulders bounced as she laughed heartily.

Jeremy finished adding food to her plate while both Geraldine and Mama Peaches eyes focused on Naima staring at Jeremy.

When Naima realized they were looking at her, she quickly picked up her phone, pretending she was receiving a text. She tapped on the screen right up until Jeremy rejoined the table.

"So Jeremy, your momma got carried away earlier thinking you were bringing her back a daughter-in-law and possibly a baby. You said you're single, but I don't buy it."

Jeremy's eyes widened as if he was appalled. He ended up chuckling at her assessment. "Ms. Geraldine, why wouldn't you believe me?"

"Because, ain't no way any seeing woman would let a handsome, good catch like you not be called for."

"Well, you better believe it."

"Why? Something wrong with you?" Geraldine snipped.

"Yeah baby, you never talk about being serious with someone. Don't tell me that you don't want to be married and don't want kids." Mama Peaches dropped her fork and propped her elbows up on the table as she steepled them in front of her and stared at him.

"Ma, all I said earlier was that I was single, and you and Ms. Geraldine have ran away with every reason but the truth."

"Well, what is it then?" Naima whispered but quickly looked away when Jeremy trained piercing eyes on her. She didn't know him or anyone else at the table had heard her. She was anxious to hear why he was single. Did he want something significant with someone at all? Because if not, that would definitely tamper her growing desire for something to evolve between them.

"Ma, you know I've always just kept to myself, focused on personal goals."

"Yeah baby, but you've achieved them," Mama Peaches said.

Jeremy let out a deep sigh thinking on how he actually hadn't achieved his biggest goal.

"But you're getting mighty close to your mid-thirties. It's time you get you a good woman, settle down and have some kids so you can enjoy them while you're actually able to."

"Ma, I've dated over the years, but nothing serious. None of them ever did it for me."

Naima' brows piqued higher. *Why hasn't a woman ever did it for him?*

"Well hell, I need you to hurry up and find one that will." Mama Peaches hissed as she grabbed her plate Jeremy was holding out to her.

He rejoined his seat.

Me. Naima was grateful that her quick responses remained in her head rather than spilling out her mouth.

"Why is all of the heat on me? Naima is sitting at the table too." He blinked in her direction. "Why don't you all have your little detective flashlights on her as well?"

"Because this is about you, boy, not her. Stay focused." Ms. Geraldine chimed in.

Jeremy shook his head before cutting up a piece of chicken and putting it into his mouth.

"So, Jeremy," Naima sat upright in her seat and

tried to fix her face before she continued on. She was certain he'd see the longing in her eyes if she didn't better compose herself. "I'm just as curious about your love life or lack thereof as these two are."

"Really?" he grinned wide. "You're gonna turn on me too? See if you ever get another meal out of me."

"Aww, don't be like that." Naima playfully whined.

"Nope." He said, standing up to his full height with his plate in his hand. "I don't care if your stomach is empty and roaring like a lion in the jungle, Jeremy's kitchen is officially closed to you."

Naima poked her lips out at him as her shoulders dropped.

"And that cute puppy dog face of yours won't work on me either."

Naima's ears perked up. Did he really think she was cute? Granted, she'd rather he considered her to be sexy, but if him thinking she was cute was a door opening for them, she'd gladly walk through it.

"Speaking of kitchens, what about yours? What restaurant will you be top chef at here, baby? I'm certain you squared that away before you even considered moving back here."

Jeremy didn't want to talk about it at the moment, but he figured he might as well get the conversation out of the way with his mother. Otherwise, she wouldn't let up on him until she knew his plans back in the city.

He sat back down. "Ma, I didn't apply to work in a restaurant here."

Mama Peaches' eyes widened. "Why not baby? You giving up on cooking because your restaurants failed?" She reached over and grabbed his hand and squeezed it.

He patted her hand on top of his. "It's nothing dire, Ma. One would think that after all I've gone through opening and trying to sustain the success of two restaurants that I would've called it quits on the whole idea. Honestly, I almost did."

Naima's heart dropped hearing him say he almost gave up on something she knew he absolutely loved.

He'd always talked about opening his own place with the cuisine and ambiance of his choice. Leaving his mark on the food world, on the world as one of the best to ever do it. To hear him say that he'd almost given up that desire made her want to jump out of her seat and throw her arms around. Provide him the comfort, solace that only a woman's touch could. But not knowing that he even saw her like that, she remained in her seat.

She would have been crushed if she would've tried to embrace him and he headlocked her as he did earlier at the store. The gesture was so platonic to her. Unlike how she wanted things between them.

He saw the despondent look in his mother's eyes and rushed to say, "But, but, I didn't and not just out of sheer will, but because the last time I was here, I came across a letter dad had left for me."

Mama Peaches hand flew up to her mouth. Her eyes glossed over.

Jeremy squeezed her hand and rubbed her forearm with the other. He shifted in his seat to get a better look at her. "He wrote it to congratulate me on the opening of my first restaurant. It detailed how proud of me he was and how he knew from when I was in your womb how I would go on to do great things in life and leave a lasting impression." He reached up and smoothed a tear away from his mom's face. "But, I never received it at the time, because well, you know he passed some time right before that first one opened."

At the mention of her late husband passing, Mama Peaches sniffled.

"It's okay, Ma. I miss him every day too. But that letter is exactly what I needed to put things in perspective."

Mama Peaches looked up at him with brightness returning to her eyes. "How so?"

"Well, it made me think like, what if none of my other restaurants succeeded because I didn't plant them where I was supposed to and with the right mission. I never wanted to open it here because I didn't want to have to live in your cooking shadow."

"Bubba, what are you talking about? My cooking shadow?" She pulled her hand from his and angled her body to get a better look at him.

Jeremy smirked. "Ma, everyone in the city of Chicago, especially Southlake Park knows how you get down on the food tip. You've cooked at numerous soup kitchens around the city and even catered a few events that had folks from other neighborhoods raving about you and when they'd get to taste your food again. You know all of the guys favored your food over mine. Even when you had me cooking for them, they'd joke that mine was okay, but not as good as yours."

Naima coughed.

Mama Peaches slowly turned her head to side eye Naima.

Naima couldn't help but laugh as she lifted her

hand up to state her piece first. "Mama Peaches, I promise you're a great cook, but in my opinion, Jeremy would always make tweaks to dishes that made them to die for." She looked at him and smiled.

He mouthed, "Thank you."

Is attention to her at the moment and the way his lips moved in silence made her hate they weren't the only two in the room. Otherwise, she might've cast her cares aside and pulled his face into her hands before placing her lips against his. But instead, she merely mouthed, "You're welcome," back. She wasn't ready to rock the boat between them just yet. If he wasn't into her like that, laying her cards out on the table with him might prove to be a failure. Make their future encounters awkward, given their family ties.

He redirected his attention back to his mother and laughed at her still side-eying Naima.

"I know what you're, doing but that's okay," she said to Naima.

Naima's eyes widened as her hands flew up in a questioning motion. "Mama Peaches, what am I doing?" Her mouth hung open in shock.

"Oh, you know what I'm talking about, what I see. The truth always comes to the light." Her side-eyeing turned into a wink, which forced Naima to cover her face and cower into herself.

"Ma, leave her alone." He chuckled. "It's okay for someone to like my food as much if not more than they like yours."

"I know that, Bubba. I'm just shocked to know you feel this way."

"*Felt*, that way. That's how I felt. In my head, I just

always saw folks coming in my place either asking if you had cooked something on the menu or questioning whether or not my food would taste as good as yours. I knew that would be too bruising to my ego back then, so I took the comparisons out of the way by trying to start up my businesses away from those who would know you."

"But now?" She lifted one of her high arching brows he inherited from her.

"Now, Pops' letter renewed my thinking on the matter, on my dream. I know in my heart that I'm supposed to open up the restaurant I always envisioned I would and with a new purpose, initiative to it."

Elbows propped up on the table, hands under her chin, and leaning over the table, Naima studied Jeremy and listened to him like it was story time in kindergarten and he was the guest author for the day. "Which is what?"

Geraldine shook her head, staring at her lovestruck granddaughter.

He perked up, prepping to tell his new vision. "Not only do I want to open a restaurant that offers healthy soul food as the top choice among other appetizing cuisine in an amazing atmosphere, but I also want to offer cooking classes. Paid ones to regular consumers. But like you mom, taking in boys in need of help, I want to provide free classes to young boys at risk. I want the classes to both offer them a different outlook on life and to create a safe haven for them off the streets. And I want to do that right here in Southlake Park."

Mama Peaches jumped to her feet and threw her arms around her son's neck as she pecked his forehead.

"Oh Bubba, that is so beautiful."

"Thanks ma."

She looked over at Geraldine. "I feel so good, I think I could win a few rounds of bingo if we go play now."

"Now, Peaches?" Geraldine's voice elevated. "I thought you wanted to finish the plans for that Bachelor Auction you came up with?"

"We can get back to that tomorrow, but tonight, we'll let these two clean up the kitchen while we go win some money." Mama Peaches started down the hall towards her room.

"Really? I have to cook and clean?" Jeremy's shrill voice crowded the kitchen

Geraldine stood up to her full five feet and eleven inches of height, pulling her purse from her lap with her. "Naw baby, you only had to cook by yourself, Naima can help you with the cleaning."

"Nana?" Naima exclaimed.

"You heard me. See you later at home tonight." She left the kitchen as swiftly as Mama Peaches had.

"Can you believe those two?" Naima said, wide-eyed, as she stared at him.

"I don't know why we even question their antics with as long as they've been going on."

"You're right." Naima laughed as she relaxed back in her chair.

Jeremy began to pick up the plates from the table. "I don't know what you're getting comfortable in that seat for, you heard your Nana, you have to help me." He stuck his tongue out at her.

The only comeback she wanted to give to his

gesture was to pull his tongue into her mouth, but unsure if he would welcome it, she figured a strong eye roll would suffice. "Whatever." She chuckled as she propped her hands on the table to help lift herself up before she began to grab plates and walk over to the countertop.

"What do you want to do, put the leftovers away or get started washing the dishes?" He asked as he grabbed a plate and began to scrape the remaining food on it into the garbage.

Her hip fell against the countertop as her arms folded across her chest. She eyed him, gauging if she should speak her mind before she forced herself to say, "What I want to know is what you were asked earlier but avoided answering it. What a woman hasn't done for you. Why haven't you been satisfied with one enough to wife her up?"

He dropped the plate into the empty sink before he turned to face her with a look of query reforming his facial features. "What?"

"What? I'm curious. I'm still trying to figure out why you," she splayed her hands towards him, "aren't taken."

He propped his butt on the sink and folded his arms across his chest and stared at her as one of his sexy, magical eyebrows lifted high. "I could ask the same of you, what exactly is your relationship status?"

She pushed herself off the counter and walked over to the sink and turned the faucet on. She held her fingers under the streaming water, gauging the pressure, before she put the stopper in it and said, "I'll wash the dishes." She dropped dishwashing liquid into the rising water.

He eyed her. "Are you going to answer my

question?"

"Nope." She didn't look up at him. "Let's just clean up this mess you made," she bumped her hip into his leg in hopes of easing the tension between them, "so I can get out of here."

He smiled. "Be like that then." He reached into the overhead cabinets nearby and grabbed Tupperware. He placed them down on the countertop. "Just know that I'll answer your question when you're ready to answer mine." He smiled and bumped her with his elbow before they fell into silence as they worked to clean the kitchen together.

Naima wasn't sure how much more of being around him and merely throwing delicate hints of her interest in him before she would either be forced to say something directly to him or leave the matter alone, but with her attraction being as strong for him as it was, she didn't even think the latter was possible.

6

"Hello, Alderman Black." Jeremy extended his hand to the man as he stepped into his office at his headquarters.

"It's been a long time since I've seen you son." Mr. Black returned a firm handshake to Jeremy before he released it.

"I know sir and it's good to see you." Jeremy followed him to the seat his hand gestured for him to sit in.

Mr. Black unbuttoned his suit jacket before he took his seat. "When my secretary, Bonnie told me that Mama Peaches said that you were back in town for good and that you had plans to open your business here, I told her to make sure you stopped by to see me."

"Which brings me here." Jeremy quickly scanned the wall of pictures behind Alderman Black displaying decades of history for Southlake Park. Having an even greater sense of pride in his roots, he fixed his gaze back on the elderly alderman. "What's going on Mr. Black."

"You know, I don't know if your mother has told

you this yet, but unless her bachelor auction can raise the additional funds needed, we'll be forced to hand these properties over to a development company that isn't too concerned about small, homegrown businesses. Not to mention we won't be able to finish beautifying Southlake Park."

Jeremy adjusted in his seat and his jaw flexed at the idea of not being able to open up his restaurant in the neighborhood.

"And it's not that they're all bad. I know that new businesses will mean more jobs for our youth and will boost commerce around here, it's just that I'd rather see the shop owners who've been here for years get to stay and budding entrepreneurs like yourself come back in and really boost this place."

Jeremy nodded at him.

"You know, so often people feel like they've made it when they get to move out of the neighborhood they've grown up in, but it says a lot more about a person's character when they realize they can bloom where they were planted."

The weight of Alderman Black's words hit Jeremy in the center of his chest. In seconds, he had put to words the revelation he had received in knowing he would flourish if he opened up his restaurant in Southlake Park.

"You are one of the roots needed in this community. I'm hoping It'd give the younger kids here now a sense of pride. Show them that we can own our own and be successful at it. It would do me proud, this community, and I'm certain your father if you open up your restaurant here."

Jeremy knew Alderman Black was right, his father

would be extremely proud that not only did he make his dream come true of owning and successfully maintaining his restaurant, but doing so in the neighborhood he had raised him and fathered countless other boys in. Harold Brighton had always been a family, community man and now more than ever, Jeremy wanted to follow in his footsteps. "Yes sir. It is my earnest desire to set up shop here, but truthfully, I won't be able to afford the long-term rent the developers want."

"I know son. No one will. But the good thing is, I have faith in that mother of yours and Geraldine that they will make it happen for Southlake Park." Alderman Black stood up from his desk.

Jeremy followed suit.

"Those two." Jeremy chuckled. He shook the alderman's hand one last time before walking out, hoping that his mother and Ms. Geraldine would indeed come through with raising enough funds from the bachelor auction.

7

"Why do those two leave out of here every time we're in here together?" Jeremy asked as he stood up from his mother's kitchen table.

Maybe because they see something you don't see, dufus. "I don't know. At least they didn't head off to bingo again." Her voice faded out as she leaned out of her chair, trying to see what he was doing with his back turned towards her.

"Dang, nosey." He chuckled. "I figured I'd make you one of my signature drinks. After the way they've been drilling you to make all of the calls you made and all else you've been doing for the auction, I was thinking you needed a pressure reliever or was I wrong?" He turned to look at her.

"No, you weren't." She couldn't help but to blush under his stare, but not being able to read him, she shifted her thoughts. "If your momma doesn't have me over here, she's over to my Nana's house or has me on the phone planning stuff. I know I haven't started working yet, but they don't have to work me like a slave. Maybe," she held onto her words as they rolled off her tongue, "if you pitched in on the planning, we'd have to spend less time working things out because there would be more people involved."

He briefly turned and gave her a "get real" stare before he got back to making their drinks.

Her lips pursed and her brow lifted as she looked at him. "Now, if you decided to be a bachelor that would be even better and I'm certain we'll make the money we hope to make."

Jeremy turned to her, laughing. "Why are you all so certain that I'll make any money as a bachelor? I'm average looking Naima."

Her face scrunched as she stared at him.

"What?"

She stood up from her seat and went to stand in front of him. "Lean down a bit."

"Why?"

"Just do it."

He acquiesced her and when his forehead was accessible, she placed the back of her hand to it.

"What are you doing?"

"Checking to see if you have a fever and that's what's sparked your delirium."

He laughed as he stood back to his full height and reached behind him to hand her the glass filled with his signature drink.

She took it from him but sniffed it.

"And why are you doing that?"

"You didn't have a fever, so maybe you dropped some chemicals in here that have you thinking, fixing your mouth to say that you are average looking."

"But I am, Naima."

"Jeremy, cut the fake humility act. You are fine and you know it." Her eyes widened, realizing that she'd flat out said it, but now that it was out there, she didn't want to take it back. She studied him, awaiting his response.

"Thanks Naima. I know you probably said that just being nice or buttering me up to be in the auction, but thanks." He turned his back towards her to grab his drink from the counter.

Is that what he thinks? She walked closer to him, ready to snatch him by the arm and force him to look at her so that she could tell him off for not seeing her, hearing what she was saying, and how he should read in between the lines. But with how close she was to him, when he turned around with his drink hand, he slammed into her. Quick on his feet, he extended his arm out to the side of him to keep from spilling his drink on her, but he wasn't lucky enough to keep her drink from getting on him.

"Oh my God. I'm so sorry," Naima said, bracing her palm on Jeremy's chest as she pushed herself off him.

She readily placed her now empty glass on the countertop next to her. "I'm, I'm so sorry." She looked at the front of his beige sweater soaked in the blood orange, delicious liquid she barely had one sip of before it ended up on him.

"It's cool," he said looking down at his shirt. He pulled the sticky material away from his skin as he looked back up at her. "You know what, just let me go to my room and change my shirt and I'll be back in here real quick." He walked past her, but then stopped in his tracks.

She turned to watch his fleeting back but ended up looking into his face. "What?"

His eyebrows met at the center of his forehead. "I just realized I don't have a room here with clothes in it to change into. This is not my house."

"Well, I'm certain Mama Peaches has a shirt big enough to fit over those muscles of yours."

"Funny." He offered her a fake smile. "She'd probably hand me duster to put on. I'll pass." The last of his words muffled as he pulled his sweater over his head.

Naima thought it would be proper for her to look away, but clearly her eyes didn't agree with that since they were trained on him as more of his abs and chest was revealed as he pulled the sweater and tank top underneath it off together. He bunched the garments up in hands as he headed back over to the countertops.

Naima touched her chin to make sure there wasn't any drool on it as a bare-chested Jeremy walked past her.

"You want me to make you another one, right?"

Her brain was working overtime, studying the many tattoos wrapping around his arms, spanning his broad and firm back all the while trying to keep her composure and not run her hands all over him. Yet he was there, shirtless, fine, and casually her asking if she wanted to another drink. Talk about being oblivious.

"Naima?"

"Hunh?" She shook her head slightly as she tried to focus her eyes on his face. "Hunh?"

"Here." He extended the drink to her. "Just don't run up on me again." He chuckled before he brushed past her to take a seat at the table. He sat down, took a sip, and said, "So, what do you think about the drink? I love it and the last spots I worked at and introduced it to the patrons, they loved it too. I just wonder how it will go over with a Chicago crowd."

"So you're not going to go get a shirt?" She remained standing, stuck in her spot near the countertop.

"No." He laughed. I already told you I'd only end up wearing one of my mom's dusters and that ain't happening." He shook his head to further his protest of the idea.

She hated to offer up her next suggestion, but she didn't think she could handle staying there with him shirtless. "With so many guys coming through here over the years, don't you think she'd have some men's clothes here? Something left of your dad's?"

"No offense to any of them, but I ain't wearing what's been handed down from boy to boy that's come through here. And if she did have something in there of my dad's, with these muscles," he patted his chest, "I would probably rip through it like the Incredible Hulk. Remember, my dad was always a slender man. Plus, if she did keep something of his, I figured it would be because she wanted to keep his scent around as long as possible. I won't interfere with that memory for a shirt I'd only need for a while. Sit down girl. Don't act like you haven't seen my boobs before."

She choked on the saliva in her mouth. "What?"

"There were plenty of times we were in the kitchen when I was younger, and I'd spill something on me and have to take my shirt off before rushing to change it. I'm certain you saw my chest back then so what's the difference now?"

She could only blink rapidly as she worked not to

state the obvious.

"Oh, I get it, you were used to my man boobs. Don't worry they're still there."

"Lies." His words made her walk forward to take a seat at the table. When she placed her drink on the table she looked at him and said. "I mean this in the nicest way, but you don't have man boobs now like you had back then."

"I beg to differ. And why do you think I have all of these tattoos?"

"I don't know. I never would've pegged you for being the type to get tattoos." She took an extended sip of her drink and found herself licking the rim of it when she was done. "This is so good."

He laughed as he watched her. "Clearly. Thanks."

"Whatever." She wiped her mouth making sure he wasn't laughing at her because any of the liquid had dribbled down her chin. "Really. You and the tattoos, I never would've put the pair together.

"Me either, but if I had man boobs back then, then obviously I was fat."

"You were big, but you were adorable."

"Ah, adorable. Girls code word for 'you're nice, maybe even nice looking but I would never date you'."

"That's not true," Naima practically shouted. She felt they were at a great point in their conversation for her to just be honest with him with how she felt about him, but when she opened her mouth to speak, he was already at it.

"Tell me anything. But for real, carrying around the weight I did and for so long, it stretched my skin out. Damaged it. When I finally decided to get the weight off after I finished getting my culinary degree, I didn't like what I saw in the mirror. I was unhappy with the stretch marks and loose skin in certain areas. Doctors said it wasn't bad enough to get skin tightening surgery.

"But getting back to my original statement, the man boobs weren't tight like I wanted them. I stumbled across a guy online with the same issue as mine. His remedy was to get tattoos. So I started getting tattoos on my chest and my arms where the stretch marks and skin was the worst, but before I knew it, I was addicted to them. Hence all of the ink you see on me." He held out his arms as if he were trying to give her a better view of the ones she could see from the front.

He guzzled down the rest of his drink and noting the shocked looked on her face, asked, "What? Why are you looking at me like I'm crazy?"

"Because I think you are. I don't see an ounce of body fat on you, but you keep referring to your chest as man boobs."

"Come here."

"What?" Her right brow lifted.

"Just come here."

She took a deep breath before she got out of her seat and took the few steps needed to stand in front of him.

He grabbed her hand. "Here, feel this." He caused the tips of her fingers to run from his nipple to the base of his pecks.

Her breathing hitched as she let his hand guide hers.

He pressed her finger deeper into his skin and then wiggled it from side to side. "See, not flabby as it used to be, but not as firm as you thought it was, hunh?" He looked up into her eyes.

"I mean, I mean-" her mouth was parched. She licked her lips as she stared down at him.

He laughed. "You can be honest. It's jiggling baby."

She pulled her hand back, chuckling. "You are crazy."

He laughed some more. "No really, back when I got the tattoos on my chest, the skin there was a lot looser, but I created a strict meal plan and a more rigorous workout life for myself and became my own plastic surgeon. I tightened my skin up to what you see now. And what about you, you have any tattoos?" He pulled on the hem of her sweater as if he were trying to lift it up.

She playfully slapped his hand away. "No."

"Good. Don't start then. I told you they're addictive. You'll end up looking like me. And forget being a corporate event planner, you'd have to become a rapper."

"You are so silly." She grinned before she turned and rejoined her seat. "Really, Jeremy, with your body, we'd make so much more money to restore the neighborhood and I don't understand why you don't want to do it since it would pretty much guarantee you the space and rate to open your restaurant slash cooking academy."

"Please don't turn in to Peaches and Geraldine 2.0." He laughed. "Being on display like that has never been my style. Y'all said y'all need my help and that's why I've agreed to be the bid catcher, the announcer. Why are you so hell bent on me being a bachelor is an even better question?" His brow lifted and he rubbed his chin as if he were Sherlock Holmes trying to solve a mystery.

Mama Peaches and Geraldine had almost walked into the kitchen but stopped short of it when they heard Jeremy's question. Mama Peaches looked up at Geraldine and said, "Asking her why she keeps pushing him to be a bachelor. How could that boy be so blind to what's right in front of him?"

8

"Oh cousin," Naima sang, using her key to let herself into Khloe's place.

Naima took note of Khloe's close proximity to Kadaris but decided to focus her energy on the task at hand. She'd orchestrated the last-minute game night to present the opportunity for her and Jeremy to get closer.

Khloe agreed to host it up in her apartment because they knew if Naima would've had it down at their Nana's house, there was a fat chance that she and Mama Peaches would've crashed the party. And although, Mama Peaches and Nana seemed to have picked up on her crush on Jeremy and were subtly trying to help him buy a clue, since it still hadn't been working, she figured a change of scenery and company just might do the trick.

Tight-lipped and narrow-eyed, Khloe pointed a steady finger at Naima and whispered, "You better be glad I love you." When she saw Jeremy warily eyeing her, she plastered on a smile and closed her front door. "So, as you can see, snacks are on the countertop and the table is already set up to play cards."

"Good. And since I'm certain you don't want Kadaris as your partner," he looked at Khloe, "I apologize for the way he and I are about to beat you both." Jeremy turned and fist bumped a smirking Kadaris. "We'll try not to beat you too bad though."

"Speak for yourself." When I play, I play to demolish my opponent." Kadaris winked at Khloe.

Khloe's fist balled up as her lips tightened and she fixed a deadly stare on Kadaris.

Naima pulled on her wrist to calm her.

Khloe faced her so that only she could hear what she was saying. "I know I said I would help you, Naima, but I can tell he's about to be in one of his moods. I can't be his partner right now. I might kill him."

Naima gripped her hand and squeezed it as her eyes widened and her lips pouted, imploring her cousin, "Please, Khloe?"

Khloe stared at Naima. Just hoping that she wouldn't want her to go through with being his partner. When she saw the resolve on her cousin's face, she knew she'd have to endure pairing up with him for Naima's sake. She took a deep breath before turning to face the guys who were knee deep in a conversation.

Naima glowed seeing that her cousin was fully onboard. She turned to the guys and clapped her hands.

Khloe pulled in a slow, hopefully calming breath and said, "Kadaris, you and I will be partners and Naima and Jeremy will pair up."

While Naima knew that it had taken much strength and restraint for Khloe's short speech, she was more concerned with how Jeremy would respond to the news. If he would have any objections to being her partner.

Currently, she couldn't read him, since it appeared he was too busy amused with the exchange between the duo.

Kadaris bore a look of shock. "Clearly, you want to be on the winning side."

Khloe tightened her lips looking at Naima. Naima discreetly put her hands in a praying motion.

"Whatever," Khloe mouthed to her.

"I'm game for the switch up. I haven't competed against Kadaris in a while. I guess it's time to remind him of who's the top dog in our friendship," Jeremy chimed in.

"Man, whatever." Kadaris brushed him off with a dismissive wave of his hand.

"And to do it with my buddy as my sidekick will be icing on the cake." Jeremy stepped next to Naima and pulled her into a headlock.

Khloe palmed her face at the sight in front of her.

"Jeremy, didn't I tell you to stop that." Naima worked to free herself from his hold, but he locked her up a little longer, tickling her. "You are such an idiot," she mumbled to herself as she stepped away from him to recompose herself.

"What did you say?" Jeremy asked.

"Nothing," she mumbled again. Knowing her whole reason for inviting him over to game night at Khloe's house, she had taken careful consideration into what she wore, how she styled her hair, and the makeup she put on.

Her yellow, off the shoulder crop top sweater allowed her creamy, dark skin to play peek-a-boo with him, and the camouflage and fitted cargo pants she wore paired with her stiletto booties cupped and lifted her butt in a way that should've had him salivating over her. But as usual, there he was, treating her like she was one of the fellas.

She hissed at Khloe as she wiped her face and patted her hair, making sure her twists were in place. When Khloe gave her a thumbs up, she stepped back closer to the rest of the crew in the room.

She avoided eye contact with Jeremy for the time being. Her mind was busy trying to figure out a way to get him to notice her other than just flat out telling him she liked him since still she worried that might ruin their friendship. Over the years, she'd seen that happen often and didn't want their friendship to suffer that same fate.

"Okay, Kadaris, you sit there." She pointed across the table from her. "I'll sit here." She touched the back of the chair in front of her. "And as long as you two are sitting across from each other, it doesn't matter which seats you take. Cool everyone?" She eyed them.

"Yes, ma'am." Kadaris stood up straight and pretended to salute Khloe.

She rolled her eyes at him and it garnered a laugh from him.

"Hold on a second. Let me make sure my partner has his head in the game," Naima said before grabbing Jeremy's hand and pulling him out of earshot of the other two in the room.

Naima kept a hold of his hand when she looked up into his eyes and said, "You ready for this? You ready for us to be a team?" The last of her words came out slowly and sensual sounding as she pulled her bottom lip into her mouth. Her bright eyes framed by her long eyelashes were wide as she stared up at him, hoping he picked up on more than what she was saying.

"Naima," he plopped his free hand on her shoulder, "it's just a game of spades. We got this. Khloe may be your cousin, but tonight, she's the enemy. Keep that in mind so we can go and beat these chumps, sport." He winked at her at the same time his mouth made a clicking sound, and his fist gently bumped her chin.

He walked away, leaving her speechless. No matter how much she pushed up on him in her own way, he still responded with the friendliest of gestures.

Is he really this clueless? Is he involved with someone and is just trying to let me down easy?

Naima didn't get the chance to ponder the questions long before Khloe summoned her to the table. "Okay," she took her seat and Khloe began to shuffle the deck of cards in her hand, "Naima, you keep score." She tilted her head towards the memo pad and pencil between the two of them. "I deal first, and we go up to five-hundred."

"Hey, why do you get to call all the shots?" Kadaris playfully fumed.

"My house, my rules." Khloe pursed her lips at him.

Jeremy shook his head. "You two are a trip."

"And so are you," somewhat defeated, Naima said below her breath as she wrote their names on the memo pad.

"You sure do a lot of mumbling under your breath, Missy," Jeremy called out to her from across the table.

She didn't look up at him. She was quite busy being annoyed with his dismissal of her, but that didn't stop her from enjoying the sound of his voice. Something she would never get enough of.

And like how she used to do back in her journaling days when she was a teenager, loving the way her name looked next to his. *Jeremy and Naima*. She had taken the time to perfect the lettering of their names and had even placed a heart above the "I" in her name.

Once done shuffling the cards and before she started dealing, Khloe looked up at Kadaris and said, "You ready? You better not mess this up. I hate losing." She narrowed her eyes at him.

"You ain't go to worry about me, just make sure you know how to count the books in your hand when it comes time for us to bid."

"I know how to play, you just make sure you know how to count." Khloe practically hissed at Kadaris.

"You two need a sitcom or, maybe you should just go out on a date and see if this animosity you have for one another is built up sexual attraction."

Naima's head popped up at Jeremy. *The nerve of him to try and hook them up when he can't even see that I'm trying to hook myself up with him.*

Khloe stopped dealing and stared at Jeremy. "You wanna play or call it a night? Because that foolishness you're talking will get you kicked out with the quickness. And when you go, take him with you." She needed her head towards Kadaris.

"Khloe?" Naima's voice was a few whimpers short of a plea.

Khloe looked over at her cousin with an "you owe me big time" stoic face.

Naima blew her a kiss and then turned to Jeremy and said, "Leave them alone and start counting your books. Remember our little pep talk."

"Of course, my dear." He gave her a fake grin.

She could only return a fake smile to him. If only he could see *her*, they could be elsewhere, solely enjoying each other's company.

Everyone got quiet around the table after Khloe dealt the last card.

Nostrils flared, jaws tensed, and smirks emerged as everyone began to look up.

"Okay, I have three books. How about you?" Khloe asked her partner.

"I have six. Want to bid nine or what?" Kadaris raised a brow at her.

They continued talking and arguing while Naima looked at Jeremy and said, "I only have two, what do you have?"

"I have five?" Jeremy responded.

"Oh, this is going to be good. Only thirteen books to win in a game and with y'all saying y'all have seven between y'all and my partner and I have nine between us, somebody is going to be set. Let the fun begin." Kadaris rocked in amusement in his seat.

"We won't be set, so enjoy your fake happiness while you can," Jeremy bug-eyed him.

Naima chuckled. No matter his attempt to mean mug Kadaris, Jeremy was still fine.

After the slapping and plops of cards on the table, and volatile mutha this and mutha that, a few rounds ended with Jeremy and Naima already in the hole.

Jeremy leaned across the table to draw closer to Naima. "Partner, what happened to you taking the advice of your own pep talk? If the past few rounds are an indicator of the rest of the game, we have to come up with a strategy. We can't go out like this. You need to loosen up? Need a massage or something?" He shrugged his shoulders.

"Yeah, that's it, Jeremy. Give her a quick massage." Khloe echoed the sentiment knowing Naima would enjoy Jeremy's touch. "Let me grab another bag and pour some more chips in the bowl." She offered to refill the snacks, hoping her absence would provide the masseur and the one being massaged some privacy. "Kadaris. I have something you could finally be of use for. I need you to grab something off the top shelf in one of my cabinets for me."

"Don't you have a step stool or something for that?" He frowned.

"Kadaris." She practically screamed at him.

"Okay. I'm coming."

"You think a massage will help you?" Jeremy looked at Naima.

"Actually, yeah. I forgot how intense spades could be." She put her hand up to her neck and rubbed it as she rolled her head from side to side.

"Hey, if it will help us win, I'm game." He stood up from his seat, rounded the table, and stood behind Naima's chair. He placed his thumbs on the nape of her neck and the rest of his hand gently around her neck.

She jumped.

He leaned down to her ear and chuckled a bit before he said, "Relax. I start from the center and work my way out, like pushing the tension outward. He deepened his grip into her flesh and her head dropped as she moaned. "You really are tense, but it's cool. It's just like kneading the dough for the crust for one of my to die for pot pies."

I wished he would shut up with the food comparisons already, or on second thought, I wouldn't reject him biting my neck.

Reveling in the feel of his warm, firm hands caressing her skin, she angled her head to one side hoping the sight of her delicate neck might appeal to him and he go beyond what only his hands were doing.

His grip extended out to the roundness of her shoulders and with the deep pressure his thumbs was applying to her shoulder blades, her head fell back in delight.

The angle allowed her to stare up at him. With hooded eyes she glanced at him hoping he was feeling the spark between them, but when he looked down at her only to pat her shoulders and say, "There, you're much better than when we started," she knew he was just as clueless then as he had been times before.

She had on her favorite floral perfume, mascara that made her lashes long and luscious, thereby intensifying the gorgeous oval shape of her eyes, burgundy matte lipstick that she knew made her lips look oh so kissable and yet the man didn't even wink at her with serious intent, let alone flirt with her.

She set up the game night thinking the camaraderie during it would help form a different bond between them because if you can't trust your partner in spades, there is no relationship to be had, but things weren't panning out the way she'd hoped they had up to that point. Nonetheless, with the fond memory of his hands massaging her, she was hopeful that as Kadaris and

Khloe returned to the table and the game got back underway things would change for her and him.

"Y'all ready to call it quits now or keep digging yourselves into a deeper hole?" Khloe asked, laughing.

"Laugh all you want to, but that last hand you all won was the last hand you won. My partner is more than ready and so am I. Ain't that right, partner?" Jeremy looked to Naima.

Naima was so lost in the authoritative way Jeremy was explaining himself to Khloe that she was oblivious to his hand in the air waiting for her to high five it.

"Don't speak so soon, bro. Your partner's mind is elsewhere. I'm hoping she carries that energy right into losing this next round. Khloe, it's your turn to deal again." Kadaris looked at her.

"I know." She grabbed the deck from the center of the table and began to shuffle them. "So, Jeremy, you've been in town, what, a little over a week? Spark up any old flames? Met a new boo?"

"Woman, that ain't got nothing to do with us winning this game. Mind your business," Kadaris cut in.

"No, you mind yours." Khloe's eyes cut daggers in Kadaris' direction.

Jeremy laughed as he began to gather his cards from the table. "Nope. I'll tell you like I tell my momma every time she asks, there's no lady in waiting. All you see is a man focused on his dream coming true."

Hearing Jeremy's declaration, Naima shook her head in annoyance. To quickly take her mind off Jeremy, she said, "What are you two bidding?"

Kadaris and Khloe looked at each other worried. Khloe shrugged. Kadaris shrugged.

"We bid four," Kadaris spoke up for him and his partner.

"You can't bid four when board is five," Naima eyed him.

"Damn," Kadaris shouted.

"Just put the little funky five down then," Khloe snipped before snarling at Kadaris.

"And how many books do you have?" Naima asked, looking up at her partner.

He looked up at her with a devious grin on his face right before he flashed her both his palms, wiggling his fingers and then held up three static fingers.

"Thirteen. Are you saying you have thirteen books in your hand?" Naima asked.

"Nigga stop lying," Kadaris smacked his lips.

"I'm not, you're just trying to deflect because that means y'all just set yourselves. And personally, there's no greater music than that right now."

"I believe you." Naima smiled at him. Her mind reeled back to an earlier part of the conversation. "Okay, so no one yet, but are you open to a relationship?" Naima couldn't help but to ask.

Jeremy chuckled as his face scrunched at her. "What? I see y'all really are cut from the same cloth. Ladies, my attention is on opening up and sustaining a successful restaurant and mentorship and oh, kicking y'all butt in spades." He plopped down the big joker. "That's right, lay down what you will. You can't beat that and you and him can no longer run from this beat down." He laid his cards down to show them he was going to run a Boston on them. "Y'all might as well just end this round here and now. Tally up the new scores, partner." He waved his hand at Naima as he looked up at the pissed faces on Kadaris and Khloe.

Jeremy kept the same arrogant demeanor round after round as he and Naima pulled themselves out of the hole they were in to win the game by one-hundred and twenty-seven points.

Khloe got up from the table with a smug look on her face. She eyed Kadaris as she started grabbing cups and the chip bowl from the table.

"Kadaris, man. Help the lady out. Go comfort your losing partner."

"Shut up, man." Kadaris popped Jeremy in the back of the head as he passed him by, going to help the fireball known as Khloe in the kitchen.

Jeremy stood up and stretched. "You see, I knew you had nothing to worry about. You didn't have money on us winning and that's why you were tense about losing, did you?"

"No, silly." She sighed.

"Good. Come on, lets' hug this win out." He stood up, went to the other side of the table and wrapped his arms around Naima and with their variances in height and her feet easily dangled above ground.

Naima wrapped her arms tightly around his neck and laid her head on chest. She loved the feel of his body against hers.

He swung her in his arms. "You are such a good sport."

She tensed in his arms at the mention of his platonic sounding compliment.

"Lady, you have got to get regular massages or do yoga or something. The tension you carry around his not good for you." He placed her on her feet. "Well guys, it's been fun hanging out with you all, but I think I'm going to head home. Between some ideas brewing in my head now and an early appointment tomorrow, I must say goodnight now."

"Really, you could stay around a little longer. Maybe we could beat them in spades again. Up to only three hundred this time?" Naima looked up at him with hopeful eyes.

"Nah, I really have to get going." He patted her rather harshly on the back before he waved at a still arguing Kadaris and Khloe in the kitchen and closed the door behind him.

Khloe walked over to Naima when she heard her door close.

"What happened, girl?"

"Nothing. Nothing as usual. Thanks for what you tried to do. Good night and good night Kadaris." Her lips poked out as she walked out the door to head to her room downstairs in her Nana's house.

Her methods up to that point of trying to get Jeremy to notice her weren't working. Even enlisting Khloe didn't do the trick.

She wondered if she needed to call in the big guns, Mama Peaches and Geraldine, or just be patient a little longer to see where the chips may fall. She just needed them to fall in her favor.

9

"You presentable?" Geraldine stuck her head in Naima's room.

"Hunh, Nana?" Naima said, looking up from her computer to her grandmother.

Geraldine stepped further into her room. "Girl, I'm trying to see if you have some clothes on. Peaches is sending Jeremy over to bring me something. I know you'll freak out if he comes in and you're looking all out of sorts. I know how sweet you are on him."

"Nana." Naima's eyes widened with embarrassment.

Geraldine cackled. "Who you think you fooling? I know you've always been sweet on him. And for the life of me, I don't understand why you ain't just told him you liked him. Could've avoided marrying that fool you did." She slowly shook her head.

Rather than tell her grandmother not to talk about her stupidity with her ex again, she hung her head. Besides, she knew her Nana wouldn't hush on the matter until she was ready to.

Geraldine walked closer in the room. "I'm sorry for always bringing him up. It just frustrates me that a ruby like you got caught up in a dirtbag like him."

Naima couldn't help but laugh at her grandmother's choice words for him, knowing she only wanted the best for her. She reached up and squeezed her grandmother's hand. "Thanks Nana."

"You're welcome, baby. If I was the old me, I would've been hooked you and Jeremy up or knocked him upside the head one to get him to see he's supposed to be just as sweet on you as you are on him, but l left my matchmaking days in the past before you came along. Yes ma'am, I tried to set all of your uncles and one of your aunties up and child, it backfired so bad, I washed my hands of the business." She motioned her hands as if dusting them of debris.

"Really?"

"Yes, indeed. So as much as I want y'all together because I want you happy and Jeremy is one of the good ones, I'll just have to let things play out between y'all the way you want them to. But for the life of me, I still don't understand why you don't just tell the man you like him, because obviously, the little hints you're throwing out, staged game night and all ain't working."

Naima covered her face in shame that her grandma knew about the game night being her plan to get closer to Jeremy.

"Child, you can uncover your face. I don't know why or how you thought you can get anything past me. I know that Khloe ain't too fond of Kadaris, so for her to invite him over, it had to be a favor for you."

The smoke alarm went off.

Geraldine shuffled towards the door. "Shoot, having a heart to heart with you made me forget about my biscuits." She closed the door behind her.

Naima closed her laptop and jumped up from the bed. She rushed to the bathroom to brush her teeth. While doing so, she was grateful that she had the twists in her head and they were still neat, otherwise, she would've had to spend time trying to make her hair look presentable.

She quickly washed her face and then ran back to her room to put on a bra and a cute sweater to complement the tribal printed leggings she'd worn to sleep.

Right as she was pulling the sweater over her head, the doorbell rang.

She snatched her room door open and yelled down the hall towards the kitchen, "I'll get it Nana."

"I know you will," the chuckling voice called back.

Naima stopped and glanced at herself one last time in the mirror in the hallway, making sure there was no morning in the corner of her eyes, before she squared her shoulders, checked her breath once more and then pulled the door open with a wide smile on her face. "Good morning."

"Good morning to you too." The dark skin man with the low fade, neatly trimmed goatee, piercing black eyes, sporting a dark brown blazer, tailored dark wash jeans and chestnut buster browns stared at Naima with a sinister smirk on his face.

"Justin?" The startled lilt in her voice and the snarl on her face were clear giveaways that his presence was a surprise and quite frankly, not welcomed.

But as usual, he ignored her signs of displeasure. "You aren't happy to see me, baby?" He reached out to touch her face, but she smacked his hand away. "Why so feisty? I thought you'd be happy to see your husband."

"Ex-husband," she hurled the words at him hoping they would send him away quicker than he came, but when she stepped in to close the door, he lodged his foot in it to prevent her from doing so.

"Is this really how you're going to treat me? After all I've done for you? After how good I was to you, this is how you treat me?" He rested his arm above his head, leaned into the door jamb and stared at her as if the salacious look he was giving her would melt the icy stare she shot back at him.

After a few more seconds of the stare down, he realized his tactic wouldn't be successful, so he stood straight up again. "Okay, let's cut to the chase, you owe me."

"I what?" Naima was flabbergasted.

"You owe me. After all the money and time I spent courting you and during our marriage, you owe me."

"You're tripping. You really need to go." She tried to close the door on him but with his foot still in the doorway and his hand resting against the door, her smaller frame was no match for his firm build and tall stature dominating hers.

"Ima."

"Don't call me that." It wasn't that she didn't like that nickname. She loved the way it sounded on Jeremy's lips, but it was always so bitter sounding off from the creep in front of her.

"Look, what do you want me to say, I'm sorry?

Sorry I didn't let go of the women I'd been banging all along even though we had gotten married? Is that what you want me to apologize for?"

"I don't want you to do a damn thing but leave me alone."

He laughed. "Look how long it took me to give you a divorce and really that was only because you managed to scrape up a good lawyer who put financial pressure on me to give it to you."

Naima gritted her teeth, wanting to sock him.

"Do you know how many models I bag on the regular? And while they are fine as ever and do whatever I want them to, I admit that there was something special about you that made me wife you. I want that back. You should just accept me as I am, a man who likes to have his cake and eat it too. Then we can get back to the life we had.

"Yeah, you may have been hurt that you caught me with your assistant, and I called you a few choice words that night, but you should also know that I miss you. I know you miss me and all the things being with me could afford you."

"I don't miss a damn thing about you or us. Would you please just leave?" She didn't want him to see her cry but fuming with anger at his audacity to show up at her grandmother's house, not to mention the things he was saying, she could feel the tears pricking her eyes.

"Baby, let me turn your pain into pleasure. I know with the way you used to scream out my name and how it's perfectly curved to my piece that no man will ever satisfy you the way I can. Come back home, Naima. I forgive you for leaving me."

"Leave."

"Not without you."

"It's been over a year since our divorce. Will you just leave?" she screamed louder.

He took a step towards her, but a hand snatching his shoulder back stopped him from getting closer to her.

Justin spun around, confused by who had the nerve to touch him in such a forceful way. "What the-" He barely had the first two words out before a man, more muscular than him was practically nose to nose with him.

"Didn't she tell you to leave?" Jeremy's nostrils flared.

"And who are you?"

"The end of you if you don't back up off of her, get off this porch and never bother her again." He flexed and contracted his fists.

"Nigga, I don't know who you are, but you don't scare me." He poked Jeremy in his temple. "That's my wife and she's coming back with me." He poked Jeremy in the head again before turned to reach for Naima.

Of course, his attempt to grab her was unsuccessful because Jeremy charged him and pinned him up against the brick wall on the porch.

"Get off of me." Justin tussled to free himself from Jeremy, but with Jeremy's forearm pinned under his neck and his left knee pushing into his right leg, he couldn't move.

"Stay away from her." Jeremy said through clenched teeth as he slipped his right hand under his left arm and applied direct pressure to Justin's throat.

Thinking that Jeremy might choke Justin to death,

Naima stepped out onto the porch and pulled on Jeremy's arm. "Jeremy, let him go."

She could see the veins in Jeremy's neck throbbing as he continued to choke Justin who was no longer fighting back. He seemed to be losing consciousness.

"Bubba, please let him go."

Her usage of his mother's nickname for him put him in a less threatening frame of mind. He eased up on the guy just enough to give him his breath back and then said, "I'm gonna let you go, but you better use the first few seconds of time to bounce out of here or else Naima won't be able to save you from me." Jeremy eyed him with caution as he released his hold on him and stepped back.

Justin buckled over and braced his hands on his knees, gasping for air. When he caught his breath, he stood back up to full 5'11 height and with head and shoulder low, charged at Jeremy as if he would try to pick him up. However Jeremy saw him coming and quickly grabbed Justin into a forward half Nelson, jacked him up with his knee in his chest, and forcefully body slammed him into the concrete landing.

Justin screamed out in pain as he tried to reach for his back, but Jeremy chicken winged his arm behind him and crouching down, shoved his knee into his side. "I don't give a damn how much pain you're in. I told you to leave when I let up off you. This time, I won't give you another chance to even think about touching her again."

"Jeremy, let him go." This time it wasn't Naima's shaky voice pleading with him but rather Geraldine's stern voice commanding him.

However, Jeremy didn't budge.

"I said let him go." She squeezed his shoulder.

The calm yet, demanding tone in her voice, similar to one his mother would've given him in the situation, snapped him out of his rage just enough to look down at Justin and say, "You better take heed to what I said."

Geraldine applied pressure to Jeremy's shoulder until he stood up and stepped away from Justin.

Still on the ground Justin wiggled and moaned in pain until he clearly gathered enough strength to roll over on his stomach and hunch to his knees before he fully lifted himself up. Staggering back, he gripped his left ribcage and looked up and pointed at Jeremy. "You done fucked up now."

Geraldine slapped him so hard in his face that he stumbled back until he fell back against the rail. "You watch your mouth." Geraldine shouted through tight lips.

Justin cupped the stinging spot on his face in shock. He looked at Ms. Geraldine with confusion. "Who the hell are you?"

Geraldine stormed at him and slapped the other side of his face harder than she did the first time. "I'm Geraldine, Naima's Nana and I never liked you." Her beady eyes seared holes into him.

Still shocked and confused that she'd slapped him twice, he said, "But you don't even know me." He rubbed his jaw, convinced that it was broken from her slaps.

"Obviously I had good reason not to. You're a coward, not a real man." She poked him in his chest. "You showed up at my door, uninvited, belittling my granddaughter, and thought she'd have no one to defend her. Well, you thought wrong. I didn't let Jeremy keep whooping on your ass because I knew my best friend would be upset if I let her son go to jail for attempted murder, but you're on my property and I have a carrying license.

"You tried to break into my house, which means I have the right to protect myself and my property. You know what, out of all the talking that's been done, you're still here. Let me just go get my piece and put an end to my granddaughter's misery. Oh, oh, he's trying to break in. He's trying to hurt me and my granddaughter. Help!" Geraldine ran in her house and behind her front door to grab her purse.

When she stepped back onto the porch and began to lift her heavy hand with the black weapon in it, Justin quickly threw his hands up in surrender.

"You coming back here?" She looked straight at him.

"No." He shook his head as he went back down one step.

"You gonna bother my Naima again?" She kept the weapon aimed at the center of his chest.

"No ma'am," his voice came out shaky.

"Good, now get the hell out of here before I squeeze the trigger on you."

Justin wasted no time in turning around and jumping the last steps until he hit the bottom landing and ran to his car down the street.

When he sped by their house, Geraldine turned to face her visibly shaken granddaughter. "You okay, baby?"

Naima's head slowly shook in disbelief. "Nana, I didn't know you had a gun."

"Child, this thing?" She wagged it in front of them forcing them to duck and bob each time she swung it past them.

She chuckled at their movements.

"Nana, you're aiming your gun at us. It's not funny. Please stop."

Geraldine aimed between Jeremy and Naima and pulled the trigger.

Jeremy flinched and Naima's eyes squeezed shut tight as she covered her ears with her hands.

Geraldine shook her head. "The only 'pow' y'all would've witnessed is the 'pow' spelled out in these bright red letters on the fabric that just popped out the nose of this gun. Silly rabbits. I see that chump nor you kids know what a real gun looks like up close."

Naima opened her eyes wide as her mouth dropped open staring at Geraldine. "Really, Nana? You had a toy gun, a clown gun? What was it going to do?"

"You see it scared him didn't you?" She turned and pointed a finger at Naima. "Now if he ever comes around here or bothers you again, which he better not because I have my second husband's piece locked in the back of my closet, you better not waste your breath talking to him. Just knee him in his balls and keep it moving. Pain and fear are the only things that register with him."

Naima shook her head.

"I love you, baby." Geraldine kissed Naima's cheek before she walked through the door, but when she made it past the threshold, she turned and looked back at

Jeremy. "And I'm glad you were here to help her."

"No problem, Ms. Geraldine." He looked at Naima. "Your nose is red. Let's get you inside." He ushered her in and closed the door behind them. "You okay?" A few feet between them gave him enough space to really look at her. Her teeth chattered and she had her arms folded across her chest like she was trying to warm herself.

"Naima," he stretched his arm out and crooked his finger under her chin, forcing her to look up at him, "talk to me."

She didn't talk but rushed to him and wrapped her arms around his waist.

He returned her embrace and rested his chin on the top of her head, and she laid her head on his chest. "You want to talk about it now or you what me to come back later?"

She squeezed him tighter.

"Okay then. I'm listening whenever you're ready to talk."

"Thank you so much for stepping in. Not sure what would've happened if you hadn't shown up," she said with her head still resting on his chest.

"As long as I'm around and it's in my power, I'll never let anything happen to you. You hear me? He squeezed her shaking body tighter.

A thought came to him. He gripped her arms and gently pushed her off him to look her in her eyes. "Ima, has he ever hit you? Be honest with me. Because if he did, I need to really go show him why he better not ever bother you again."

She shook her head. "No Jeremy, he didn't."

"Good." He pulled her back into him and rubbed

her back. "So is that why you never wanted to talk about him before today, because he was a complete jerk to you?"

"No. I didn't want to talk about him because then I'd have to explain why I was an idiot for being with him."

"Don't beat yourself up. I know how dudes can be. Pretenders until they get tired of putting on the show and when they get tired of acting, the real them comes out. Most often they don't change, the woman has to decide to walk or stay. You walked away."

"Yeah after a long divorce battle with him."

"That's okay. You were able to cut ties with him and that's what matters the most."

She pulled back from him. "You hurt?"

"Nah, I'm straight."

"Okay. But don't try to be all macho on me. If you're hurt somewhere, let me know."

She stared up at him. "I guess I messed up your morning hunh? All you did was come over to get something for your mom and you literally ended up having to fight my battle." She lowered her head, ashamed that he knew how much of fool she'd been and for whom.

"Stop apologizing. I'll always be here for you. And now that we're both back in town, I just have to step my brotherly duties up even more since he may still be lurking around."

Her head snapped up at him. "Brotherly? You see me as your sister?" Her voice was no short of spite.

"Hold on tiger." He chuckled. "We've only ever been platonic friends. Am I supposed to see you any other way? Put the moves on you because you're such a cutie only to have it ruin our friendship because you don't want me, never have?" That right eyebrow of his lifted high on his face. He studied her body language as he awaited her response.

Any other lovestruck person would've used his questions to come clean, but not Naima.

He'd call her cute, but he'd also said it was his brotherly duty to protect her. His words weren't exactly clear that he wanted more with her. She didn't want to cause friction between them.

And although she'd much rather engage him in a comforting, revealing kiss that attested to her not being anything near a sister to him, she didn't feel it was the right time to explore that avenue given what had just happened. Because like he said, they both lived in Chicago now, the wrong move on her part could permanently alter things between them and not in a good way.

"Never mind." She smiled for good measure. "I'm sure you want to grab what you came for so you can be on your way."

He looked back at the door as if someone would walk through it and then looked back at her. "Nah, I think I'll stay around a little while longer just in case old boy didn't get the memo Ms. Geraldine and I FedExed him. I'll just call my momma and tell her I won't be back for a while."

"Okay." As he stood in the hallway, making the call, Naima took the time to head to her room to recompose herself. She passed on the opportunity to come clean to him yet again. She had no one to blame but herself, yet that didn't stop her from sulking as she closed her door behind her. She'd get back out to Jeremy as soon as she perked herself up.

10

Jeremy inhaled a deep sigh before he used his key to enter his mother's house. He knew the trio was there finalizing plans for the bachelor auction. He would have loved to avoid them while they planned since he knew they would still try to get him to be a bachelor, but his need to check on their progress with raising enough money to revitalize the neighborhood trumped his discomfort of their insistence.

He walked through the door and closed it quietly behind him. Rather than make a grand entrance, he wanted to surprise them, but he was pleasantly surprised by the smell wafting in the air.

Granted he was a master chef and could cook whatever he wanted, but there was nothing like going to his mother's house knowing she knew how to throw down in the kitchen and could satisfy his palette.

He hung his jacket on the coat rack near the door before he mimicked tiptoeing down the hall towards the kitchen. Not trying to eavesdrop, but he couldn't help it as he stopped short of the kitchen when he heard

Geraldine say, "Girl, I don't know why you won't just tell the man how you feel. Let the chips fall where they may."

"I'm with Geraldine-"

"Nana and Mama Peaches, can we please talk about something else?"

He heard the despair in Naima's voice and knowing how the ladies could go on and on, he decided to rescue her from the duo when he made himself visible in the kitchen. "Ladies, how are you doing?" He spread his arms wide as he went around the room quickly hugging and kissing each of them.

His hug with Naima was different than anyone before. Whereas she would normally embrace him and seem to sink into him, she didn't even return the gesture.

But he figured that if she was having man troubles, that stood to explain why she wasn't her usual self with him.

"What do we have here?" He stood over the stove lifting lids and looking in the pots. "Ooo, grits." He looked back at his mother. "Do you have green onions and shredded cheese?"

"Of course, Bubba."

He shook his head, chuckling. "You think you'll ever stop calling me Bubba?"

Mama Peaches turned in her seat to look at him. "You ever gonna stop being my son?"

His face scrunched up as he looked back at her. "That's not possible."

"Well then, that's your answer." She turned back towards the notebook she had in front of her.

He grinned as he raided the refrigerator for the

garnishes he wanted.

He reheated his bacon in the skillet on the stove and soon sat down with a bowl and saucer in front of him.

"You never do simple with your food, hunh?" Sullen, Naima chimed in, staring at the stellar display of food. "Are you going to actually eat it or just take a pic to post on the gram."

"Ha ha." He chuckled sarcastically. "I'm definitely eating all of this." He hovered his hand around the top of the bowl before he winked and dipped his spoon into the grits. He put the grits in his mouth and Naima couldn't help but stare at him satisfying himself with scoop after scoop of the grits and taking healthy bites of his bacon.

Although she definitely wanted more than an eye-rolling, toe-tingling, wall-climbing sexual experience with Jeremy, she couldn't help that that's where her mind often went when she stared at him.

The man was gorgeous.

And the fact that all of his fineness was attached to an equally great guy made her lower region tingle on more occasions than she cared to discuss with anyone.

Too bad the moron doesn't feel the same about me.

Her eyebrows furrowed as she looked down at herself for a second. *Am I not sexy?* She pulled on her fitted chenille sweater and ran her fingers across the rips in her jeans as if her outfit was an indicator of her sex appeal.

She quickly dismissed the wayward thought, knowing that she was beautiful inside and out.

"Naima?" Jeremy walked from the sink where he'd left his dishes and over to her.

"Hunh?"

"I've been trying to get your attention for a second." He gripped the base of her neck with deep, circular motions and leaned down to speak in her ear. "You alright?" His breath tickled her ear and the deep timbre of his voice sent a sensual chill down her spine.

Her eyes fluttered closed and she whispered out, "Yeah, I'm fine."

"You sure?" His lip grazed her earlobe and she pulled her bottom lip into her mouth.

She nodded in response. She didn't trust how her voice would sound.

"Remember, I'm here for you if you need me." He rubbed her arms a few times before he returned to his seat at the table.

"Dumb," Geraldine said shaking her head and pursing her lips at Naima.

"Just plain dumb," Mama Peaches said eyeing her son.

"What?" Jeremy eyed both of the older ladies with warranted suspicion.

When they didn't respond, he got down to the reason he had come there. "Ladies, I need to know how things are looking. Does it look like you'll get the rest of the money needed to finish the neighborhood renos from the bachelor auction."

"We'd have it if you'd just be a bachelor already," Mama Peaches scoffed.

Jeremy lifted out of his seat high enough to scan the paper his mother had in front of her. He pointed towards it and said, "From the looks of the check marks next to names on that list, you have more than enough bachelors to make the money you need. Besides, it's not like your funds will solely come from auctioning off the bachelors. Naima told me that a company agreed to generously multiply the amount you get for each bachelor. You all are good with the amount of bachelors you have. I thought me agreeing to be the bid catcher was sufficient for that night?" He sat back down in his seat.

"Bubba, now you know I love all of the boys that came through here over the years, but none of them are as fine as you."

Naima chuckled.

Mama Peaches snapped her neck in Naima's direction and said, "You're saying my boy is not handsome?"

Jeremy cocked his neck at Naima.

"Oh, he's more than handsome. I'm not laughing at that, just amused that you used that same line on all of them to coerce them to participate."

Mama Peaches squinted at Naima. "You little snitch you," she said through gritted teeth. You're supposed to be on my side, remember?"

"I know, I'm sorry. But you're just so funny," Naima covered her mouth, trying to hide her smile since Mama Peaches seemed intent on staring her down until she found the matter less amusing. "Okay, I'm done," Naima said with a barely straight face and held her hands up in surrender.

"Ma, me being a bachelor conversation is supposed to be dead. I'm just here to make sure you all are making progress because it's the only way I'll be able to afford setting up my restaurant here in Southlake Park."

Mama Peaches whipped her neck in his direction.

"What do you mean? I thought you had all of that stuff settled before you moved back here."

"Not quite." He sighed. "As with the others, opening a restaurant, stepping out the ledge to be an entrepreneur, a business owner is risky. I'm going to open my restaurant, the issue is just whether or not I get to do it here or in another part of town."

"Well, why is here not the only option?" Mama Peaches asked.

Jeremy huffed and rubbed his head before he looked up at them. "I didn't want to say anything to you because I didn't want you to go all Peaches Brighton on the people down at the development headquarters or even the alderman, but if you all don't raise the funds that you promised him, he'll be forced to the sell the commercial storefronts in the neighborhood to a real estate development company. The rent will then be way out of my price range, not to mention for the other businesses still existing in the neighborhood and for future ones who would want to come in.

"If we don't keep that development company's hands off Southlake Park, I'm certain you'll see a Starbucks down the street instead of Southlake Park Java that the Johnson's have owned for over a decade. And we can definitely kiss the market goodbye. I'm certain one of the big chain grocers will have no problem buying up that whole side of that block to capitalize on this reemerging neighborhood. I can't afford to open up here with that development company's prices and even if I did, I wouldn't be able to sustain its existence. We have roots here and we need to keep it that way."

"Which is all the more reason why I don't

understand why you won't be a bachelor. What we earn from you could be the final bid needed to reach our goal amount."

"Ma, you just don't get it." He slammed his fist down on the table.

Mama Peaches eyes bucked at him. "Have you lost your damn mind? Slamming on my table and talking to me like that!"

"Let me get out of here." With uneven breaths and throbbing temples, Jeremy jumped up from his seat and headed towards the front door in spite of his mother calling after him.

"Jeremy Nathaniel Brighton."

Naima rushed after him and caught him by his arm before he stepped out the door. "Jeremy, what is going on?"

He paused to regain his composure before he turned to look back at Naima. The compassion in her voice was more than enough to keep him in place.

"Talk to me." She squeezed his hand, but he remained silent. "I remember, not too long ago," she smirked, "you badgered me until you found out what my ex had done."

He pursed his lips at her. "I badgered you about it?" His forehead scrunched. "I only found out about him when I overheard him telling on himself and then you filling me in the rest of the blanks on your history with him."

"Tomatoe, tomato." She shrugged her shoulders.

"Whatever." His stoic demeanor finally softened, and he smiled at her.

"Really, Jeremy, you kept reminding me how great

of friends we are and that I could talk to you about anything, I think it's time you trust me with the same. Why are you so dead set on not being a bachelor and why did you almost commit suicide talking to your mother like that?"

"I did, didn't I?" He looked past Naima as if he would see his mother appear in the hallway. With no one else there but the two of them, he looked back down at her and said, "Come sit in my car with me and I'll tell you. My adrenaline has worn off and I'm kind of scared that she'll come storming down this hallway with a frying pan aimed at my head at any moment."

Naima laughed. "You're silly."

"But you know I ain't lying. Let's go." He pulled on her hand.

"Oh, but it's cold out there, let me grab my jacket." She turned to head back to the kitchen, but he kept a firm grip on her hand.

"No. Here, take mine." He wrapped the jacket in his hand around her shoulders. "Plus, I pressed the remote start on my car when I was storming down the hallway, it should be warm in there by now."

"Okay."

When seated in his car, he toyed with the buttons for radio stations on the console.

"Jeremy, talk. Help me make sense of what you want to accomplish versus what you won't do." She reached over and grabbed his hand.

His head fell back against the headrest and he let it roll over until he faced her. "You promise you won't laugh if I tell you?"

"I promise." She squeezed his hand for good

measure.

Being in such a confined space with him, the old school 90s R&B softly playing through the car's speakers, the scent of his cologne, and his firm grip on her hand, had her cursing herself out in her head. *Why did I agree to come out here with him? How can I focus on what he might tell me when all I want to do is kiss those soft pink lips of his, climb into his lap and-*

"Ima, are you listening to me?"

"I'm sorry, what did you say?" Her eyes blinked rapidly.

"I said it happened in the eighth grade." He pulled his dark brown eyes away from her to stare out the front window. "I don't like being judged."

"What?" Still holding on to his hand, she tucked her foot under her and turned to face him. "You won't be judged. You'll be ogled, desired."

"You see it that way, but I see it like I'll be stared at. Picked apart as the women decide if I'm worth their bids. I'm not down with that."

"I'm still not understanding why you're thinking of this in a negative way."

"If you notice, on my social media pages, I don't have many full body shots of me in my food videos and pics."

I know, which is why I was floored when I saw you for the first time in years.

"The ones you can see my face in, were shared by others who posted them."

I know, hence my scavenger hunt for pics of you on there.

He took a deep breath. "I never told my mom and dad about this, not even Kadaris, but it happened during the eighth-grade talent show. This particular group of boys had always teased me because of my size, but I somehow managed to brush off what they said until that night. Remember you had a crush on Ralph Tresvant?" He chuckled. "You always sang his parts and had these dreamy eyes whenever his part came on."

"Yeah." She lied. She didn't have the dreamy eyes because of Ralph Tresvant but rather because whenever the songs would come on, Jeremy sang Ralph's part with all he had in him. It was Jeremy she was star struck by, not the singer.

"Well, you know I had a little voice back then."

Sir, your singing voice is just as sexy as your talking voice.

So, I was backstage rehearsing my performance and those same punks who had been trying to bully me all year, dogged me out and pointed at me saying I was a clown for thinking that the girls would scream for me the way they did for New Edition. They harped on how fat I was."

She rolled her eyes, annoyed that the boys had treated him that way. He was always beautiful to her.

"Before that, I wasn't necessarily insecure

about my weight, but their taunts really fell on me that night and it made me think, would I really make the girls scream for me the way they screamed for Ralph or any of the others in New Edition?" He slipped his hand from hers and she immediately missed the connection their hands locked together provided her.

He plopped his hands on the steering wheel. "I thought back on that year and if I even had a girl flirt with me."

Me. She shouted in her head.

"And when I couldn't recount one, I pretended like I was sick so my momma and daddy could take me home. After that, I really buried myself in food and cooking. It was a solitary activity and I found solace in it."

"I'm sorry you went through that, but look at you now. You're not that chubby, insecure boy anymore."

He looked at her with amusement. "Too scared to call a spade a spade. I was fat. Say it, I was fat."

"To me you weren't," she mumbled.

"I know you're just trying to be nice, but the truth is I was fat."

Averting eye contact when asking her next question, she played with the frayed thread on her jeans. "So is that why you look the way you do now?"

"How do I look now?" He chuckled.

"You know, all muscular."

He laughed heartily. "I admit, I was kind of working towards my revenge body at first, but the more I got into working out and eating right, I realized I was doing it for my health and longevity. Plus, there was no way I would be around long enough to keep enjoying my passion, cooking, if I would've kept eating the way I was."

"I get that and I'm happy for you and proud that you took the necessary steps to be the best you can be. Don't you think being a bachelor would be the best thing to ensure that you actually get to open up your restaurant here?"

"Are you a secret agent for them?" He squinted his eyes at her.

"No, silly." She shoved him in the shoulder. *I want to bid on you.* "No, you know what, never mind. You ready to go back in there and apologize to your mother? You won't be a bachelor, but we can go in so you can practice being the best bid catcher to ever do it."

"Go back in there?" He pointed past her to the house. "You mean am I ready to go back in there and get my head chewed off?"

"That too."

"I guess." He let out a nervous laugh before he turned the car off and got out of the driver's seat to open her car door.

11

"I'm really glad you agreed to host this with me, Naima. We probably wouldn't make much money if I had to be the one giving the description of the men and talk them up to the audience. Glad I only have to call out current bid numbers and ask for more."

"You would do good by yourself too." Naima stood in front of him with her hands behind her back.

"Please, me telling how sexy another man is, how well his suit is fitting him, how dazzling his smile is, or how his muscles are bulging? Nope, not me," he said with a straight face as he rested his back against the wall with his foot propped against it.

Jeremy stared at Naima for a beat.

She couldn't quite read the look in his eyes so she asked him, "What?" on the breath of a nervous laugh.

"Has anyone ever told you, have I ever told you how good you look in yellow?"

"What? No." Her words came out quick and high pitched.

"Ima, you are wearing the hell out of the dress.

With the way it's melted against your skin, I don't know how you got in it or how you plan to get out of it, but it looks good on you."

"Thank you," she whispered, smiled and averted eye contact with him.

"I got it." He lifted off the wall. "You're rocking that because that guy I overheard y'all talking about that one night will be here?"

"What?" Naima's eyes widened with confusion.

"I wasn't trying to eavesdrop but I came in on the end of a conversation where it sounded like you hadn't told a guy you were feeling him, but Ma and Ms. Geraldine were telling you to just share with him how you feel. Is he one of the bachelors?" His eyes widened with mirth. "You gonna bid on him? You trying to get some tonight?" Jeremy shoved her in her shoulder.

Her face scrunched up in embarrassment and annoyance. "What? No."

"Wait, the only guys that are bachelors tonight are ones who came through my house. Is that why you were over all of the time? You were hoping to catch his eye back then? Y'all ever hook up? Kept up with each other over time? Aside from when you were married of course."

"You know what, you're a real idiot." She tried to walk off, but he grabbed her by the wrist.

"Naima, what did I do?"

"Jeremy and Naima, come on. It's time to get this party started." Ms. Geraldine clapped her hands and shimmied as she walked up to them.

Still holding onto her wrist, Naima refused to turn to look at Jeremy. *Why do I still want him even though*

106

he's so clueless and shows no signs of wanting me? But can I really be mad at him if I haven't been honest with him? Her back and forth battle in her mind made her inhale and exhale a deep breath before she turned back to him with a faux smile on her face. "Nothing, Jeremy. Nothing at all."

"Come on you two," Ms. Geraldine called after them again.

Naima pulled her wrist from his hold and walked past him and with her eyes fixed on her grandma, said, "Coming Nana."

Jeremy stared at her as she walked past waiting for her to say more as to why she adamantly called him an idiot. When he no longer saw her in the hallway, he realized she wouldn't tell him, so he made his feet follow the path hers had until he joined her on stage.

***

"Are you all having a good time tonight?" Naima asked the crowd.

"Yeah."

"Keep the cuties coming."

"I need another one to take home with me tonight."

"Oh, yeah."

The string of comments mixed in with catcalls and the other cheers sent the crowd in another uproar of laughter before Naima chose to speak up again. "Okay, ladies. We're so glad you've been enjoying yourselves. Your gracious bids have put us so close to our goal for the night. Let's see if the last two bachelors of the night will put us at or push us past our goal. Keep those giving hearts pumping."

"Is that fine auctioneer one of the last bachelors to be bid on?" A busty, tall woman stood to her feet and yelled out with her eyes trained on Jeremy.

He cleared his throat as he adjusted the bow tie around his neck. He spoke through a tight lip smile when he looked over to Naima and said, "Let's hurry this up so I can get off this stage before she actually comes up here. I don't like the way she's been eyeing me all night."

Me either. Naima quieted the jealous thoughts in her head as she yet again pasted a fake smile on her face to offer to Jeremy.

Not wanting to anger the women in the crowd, she chose not to inform them that Jeremy wouldn't be a bachelor, but instead pumped herself back up to smile at them and say, "Ladies, I'm certain the next bachelor will more than grab your attention and make you grab your wallets and credit cards. Up next, we have Charles Markham. Thirty-six and single, he's originally from Chicago but now settled and dominating the stock market in Boston." She turned to face the door he would be coming from. "Ladies, the handsome stud that is Charles."

He barely made it to center stage before women began whistling at him and clapping loudly. Many had firm grips on their paddles just waiting for Jeremy to start the bidding.

"We'll start the bidding at 100. Can I get 100?" Jeremy was barely heard before the crowd of women took over.

"500!" The arm of a stout light-skinned woman shot

up.

Jeremy pointed to her.

"700!"

Jeremy repeated the last number called and pointed to the appropriate woman as quickly as the numbers rang out.

"1000!"

"3000."

A hush fell over the crowd as women began turning in their seats looking for the woman with the assured voice who had placed such a high bid. When their eyes fell to the tall and full-figured, mocha-skinned woman holding her white paddle just above her head, they all turned around and pursed their lips knowing they wouldn't bid above that.

"3000 going once?" Jeremy scanned the crowd, "going twice?" He looked over the crowd once more, when no one lifted a finger let alone a paddle, he dropped the gavel down on its companion and said, "Sold to the lady in red."

"I hope she gets her money worth from him." One woman on the front row did a poor job of whispering to the lady next to her.

The lady next to her leaned into her said, "Girl, judging from the bulge in his pants, I think she'll be more than satisfied if it gets down to that."

Their shoulders bounced as they chuckled.

Charles walked past and fist bumped Jeremy. Jeremy then leaned down to Naima and said, "See why I didn't be a bachelor. I would've been just a piece of meat. The hope of a good one-night stand." He stood back up to full height and looked out onto the crowd.

Naima looked up at him and her mind wandered. *I'd start with a one-night stand with you, but there'd definitely be more nights and days with us.*

"Hey, would you get out of Lalaland long enough to finish hosting?" He chuckled.

She announced the last bachelor, Christian Knight, the only one of Mama Peaches' boys to pursue sports and make into the majors. All of them knew he was a pro baseball player and his presence on stage was met with over the top applause and salacious cheers.

Standing back watching the last bid take place, Naima was bummed that she didn't get to bid on Jeremy and use the event as a segue into hopefully building something more romantic with him.

After Christian had been bid on, Naima said, "Okay ladies, we absolutely appreciate you all for helping to make this night as fun as it has been. The DJ will amp up the music and you all can dance and party once we leave the stage, but before we get to that, we'd like to introduce the masterminds behind this night to give the final remarks and hopefully share that we've reached our goal." She looked to the right of her to see that Mama Peaches and her nana standing nearby.

She handed the mic to Mama Peaches and then went and stood by Jeremy who had stepped back from his podium and had been inching his way back off the stage.

"Ladies, you all have truly made this night a success." Mama Peaches waved a white envelope in the air as she wagged her tongue. "But before we share how much we raised tonight, we do have one more bachelor up for auction."

"Yes! I just knew I wasn't going home alone tonight. Ladies," the speaker quickly looked around the room, "don't bid too high on him. Let me take him home tonight," the slender and short woman yelled from the middle of the room.

There was a mixture of chuckling and head shaking from other attendees in the crowd.

Jeremy flipped the paper of names over and over in his hands. All the men on it had been bid on. He leaned down to whisper to Naima. "You know who she's talking about?"

"No," Naima said honestly.

"This one here was kind of shy to do it, but I know for a fact that there's a woman here ready to bid on him. I'll take her happiness over his anger. Besides, he's my son, he'll get over it."

Jeremy's eyes widened as the spotlight shined on him.

His face scrunched up as he warily eyed his mother. He began to shake his head and hold his hands up in protest as she neared him.

He looked at Naima and said, "Did you know about this?"

She looked up at him. "No. I'm just as shocked as you are."

He looked back at Mama Peaches. "Ma," he huffed, "I love you, but I'm not doing this."

"Boy, will you just trust me?"

There wasn't much protest for him to give at that point given the strong grip she had on his hand and the tight-lipped way she looked at him. Grace and mercy had saved him from her wrath the night he stormed out of her house, he wasn't sure favor would circle back around for him so soon.

His nostrils flared as he let her drag him out to the center of the stage.

"Wooo. I've been waiting on you all night long, daddy," A lady hollered from the back of the room.

"Girl, you better hope your pockets run deeper than mine, otherwise he'll be taking me out on the surprise date he's planned," a more demure woman standing along the left wall said.

Mama Peaches put the mic back up to her mouth and said, "Ladies, obviously you all didn't hear me, I'm doing this for one woman."

Jeremy's eyebrow shot up in her direction. "Who?" he mouthed to her.

"I'll start the bidding at 100. Can I get a 100?"

Paddles flew up all around the room.

Geraldine cut behind Mama Peaches and walked over to Naima. "Gon' head and put in your bid." She winked at her.

Naima's mouth fell open. When it registered what they were masterminding, she hissed, "Nana."

Geraldine shook her head. "Lawd you are one hard-headed child." Geraldine grabbed Naima's hand and raised it in the air and said, "100."

Smiling hard, Mama Peaches picked up the gavel from the podium and slammed it down as she shouted, "Sold."

"No fair," The first woman who thought she would be taking Jeremy home with her that night whined.

"Get over it," Mama Peaches said into the mic. "We've now exceeded our goal."

The crowd erupted with laughter and cheers.

"DJ, get this party started," Mama Peaches directed before she placed the mic on the podium.

Jeremy spun quickly on his heels and stared at the trio not standing too far from him. He walked over to them. "Ladies, what is going on?"

"Yes, what is going on?" Naima's hands went up to her hips as she stepped next to Jeremy to stare at Mama Peaches and Geraldine.

"What happened is, I got tired of dumb and dumber, which would be you two carrying on like you have these past couple of weeks," Mama Peaches spoke up.

"Ma, what do you mean?"

"She means Naima has always had a crush on you," Geraldine chimed in.

Naima covered her face in embarrassment.

"Is that true?" Jeremy's neck snapped to look at her. He didn't believe what he was hearing.

"Yes." Geraldine poked him in his chest. "She's been flirting with you since y'all got back and you haven't picked up on any of it. Like Peaches said, dumb and dumber. She was too scared to tell you how she really felt about you and you were too slow to see how she was reaching out to you in her own misguided way. Or did you see it and was just pretending like you didn't? Think my baby isn't pretty enough for you?" Geraldine poked him in the chest, causing him to stumble back a little.

"What? I think she's beautiful. I just never knew she liked me. I used to have a crush on her back in the day, but I figured she didn't like me because of my size so I abandoned my interest in her."

Naima's face marred with frown lines. She locked eyes with Jeremy, but neither one of them said anything.

"Looks like y'all have some things to discuss then." Geraldine pursed her lips at the end of her words.

"Well Deen, now that that's finally out in the open and we met our goal, let's go partay!" The women high fived each other as they walked behind the curtains, dancing.

When the women were out of their sight, Jeremy pulled Naima behind the curtains to provide more privacy for them. "So, were they right, you've always had a crush on me?"

Naima forced her gaze to the floor rather than on him.

"Hey." He lifted her chin with his finger crooked under it.

She bit the inside of her mouth as she finally looked up at him.

"Haven't we been constantly telling each other these past few weeks that we can talk to each other about anything and that we can trust each other?" He didn't even let her answer before he said, "so let's not clam up now."

"Yeah." She smacked his hand away from her face. "I always have, but you were just too blind to see it."

"What?" he overexaggerated his question as his hands flew up and walked around her to face her rather than talk to her back since she had turned it on him. "How was I supposed to know you liked me if you didn't tell me?"

"Come on Jeremy, I was in that kitchen with you almost every day I was in town on school vacations."

"And your mere presence was supposed to clue me in? I thought you just liked to sample my cooking and like I said earlier, I thought maybe you came over so often because of one of the other boys staying there."

"No." She poked him in the chest. "I came there for you." She kept poking him in the chest.

He grabbed the hand she had been poking him with and used it to pull her closer to him right before he gripped the base of her neck with his other hand and massaged it.

His actions made her look up at him.

"I'm going to kiss you right now, is that okay?"

She didn't use words to answer him but rather inched on her tiptoes and wrapped her hand around his neck, pulling his face down until his nose tickled hers.

She parted her lips and he accepted the gracious invitation by covering her lips with his.

His hands fell to the small of her back and he pulled her closer as he titled his head giving him better access to explore the intricacies of her mouth.

Her tongue collided, tangled, and dueled with his as she sought to make up for missing out on moments like that with him over the years.

Jeremy never knew he enjoyed kissing until he kissed Naima, so it was her who had to pull back from him first when she needed to catch her breath.

Her chest heaved as she watched him stretch back out to his full height. When he did so, she quickly leaned back into him and gripped his neck forcing him to lock lips with her again.

He eagerly obliged.

Moments passed with them engaging each other in

such an intimate way. This time around, Jeremy was the one to pull away first. The right corner of his mouth lifted, and his eyes smiled as he stared at her. "I could keep kissing you forever, but I think we need to talk about this." He pointed between the two of them.

"You sure?" her voice was heavy with lust as she smiled at him and tried to go in for another kiss.

"Yes, Ima." He chuckled as he patted her butt. "I could see why you didn't tell me you liked me when we were younger. Teenage nerves, plus the fact that we didn't even live in the same state would've prevented us from really blossoming in that way, but why didn't you say anything to me these past few weeks?"

She pulled away from him. "You're right. I liked you so much back then that I was too nervous to tell you that I liked you and have you break my heart with a no, but what was I supposed to say now Jeremy, I really like you? Always have and I want to be more than friends with you?"

"Uh, yeah."

"You say that now, but for you not to pick up on my flirting-"

"Ima, first off, you really need to work on your flirting skills."

"Whatever." Her eye roll turned into a laugh. "You were always putting me in headlocks and even said you were doing your brotherly duties protecting me, I figured you really didn't see me like that. It still didn't stop my feelings for you, but with us both living here now, I didn't want to expose myself to you like that, you not like me and then things be awkward between us moving forward."

"Women really do over think things."

"Hey." She playfully punched him in the arm.

"I'm just saying, with the time we've been spending together over the past few weeks, we've been reacquainting ourselves with one another, you should've just told me. And we would've dealt with our feelings right away rather than the way things happened tonight."

"And why didn't you say anything to me back then if you had more than a platonic interest in me?" She bit the inside of her jaw, awaiting his response.

"I don't know, same reason as you, I guess. You were so pretty and cool and down to earth, I wasn't sure a girl like you would like a chubster like me. I didn't want to try my hand either and ruin our friendship. I really enjoyed being around you." He swiped his hand over his face. "When I walked in the kitchen and I saw you for the first time, I was like damn, Naima is finer than a frog's hair."

She chuckled. "Whatever silly."

"For real. That came to mind among a few other thoughts I won't share just yet."

Her cheeks grew warm.

"But I guess my mind quickly went back to when we were younger and how I figured you never liked me then so you wouldn't like me now."

"Like I've said, idiot."

"Let the duo tell it, we're," he pointed between the two of them, "dumb and dumber." They both laughed.

Naima's laughter sobered up and she said, "So you mad at them for outing us?"

"I mean, I'm glad I know how you feel about me. I'm glad I've tasted your lips."

She blushed.

"I just don't like the way they did it. I would have rather it be done in private. But then again, it may not have ever happened, so I guess I'm glad they did." He swiftly pulled her into him by the small of her back and pecked her lips.

She pulled back enough to look at him. "I mean, I eventually would've told you. My feelings were getting too strong for you the more I was around you. I was just waiting for the right time."

"They made it the right time tonight, hunh?"

"They sure did."

"So I went from being the bid catcher to a bachelor after all tonight, hunh?" His grip of her strengthened.

She wrapped her arms around his neck. "Yup, but I'm looking to take you off the market. You okay with that?"

"Am I okay with that?" His voice pitched high. "Hell yeah. You are beautiful inside and out. And I know it may have annoyed you over the years, but I believe the friendship that we cultivated when we were younger and got back to when we both made it back to Chicago has given us a solid foundation to build on. So, I'll always see you as my friend too. Having that frame of mind is a shoo-in for a successful romantic relationship. And don't get it twisted, just because you won me for the low, doesn't mean I'm cheap. Remember that."

She chuckled. "Shut up and kiss me again."

My pleasure. He grabbed handfuls of her butt as he devoured her lips and tongue in a kiss so hot, he questioned if he could bottle it up and sell it as a spicy herb.

6 months later…

"Come in."

Naima peaked her head in before she stepped into his office. "Hey you. I was looking for you."

He stood up from the chair behind his desk and walked around to the front of the big wooden fixture. He smiled at her in her yellow sundress as she walked towards him.

"You okay?"

"Yeah this is just still surreal.

What? Did something happen to send you in here to hide in the dark on your opening night?" There was no mistaking the concern in her voice as she reached up to caress his face.

He chuckled. "No, just the opposite." He perched his butt on the desk and pulled her in between his open legs. "I had to step away from everyone for a second so I wouldn't look like a fool jumping up and down or clapping in excitement."

"Oh. So you're in here for a good reason?"

"Yes, and you being in here with me now makes the moment even better." He gently gripped her chin, holding her face in place as he puckered kisses to her lips."

She smiled as she accepted his adoration of her.

She gathered on her tiptoes, gripped the nape of his neck with clasped hands and pulled his face closer to hers. The desirous look in her eyes, just before their lips touched, let him know that she expected much more than the chaste pecks he'd recently given her.

He smirked as he wrapped his arms around her and

pulled her into him, causing her breasts to be flush to his chest. He loved the feel of her against him. He rested his chin on the top of her head as he held her tightly.

"Mmmh," she whined. "I wanted a kiss."

He laughed. "I know you did, but I just wanted to hold you for a second."

She squeezed him tighter. "You sure you okay?"

"Of course." He pulled away from her to look her in the eyes. "Call me crazy or even clairvoyant if you want to, but I just know that I'll succeed this time around." He tickled her side.

She giggled and squirmed in his arms as she said, "You will."

"And that's not the only reason I'm okay, scratch that, I'm more than okay, I'm great. I'm really happy." He paused, knowing she would readily ask him why, but when all she did was stare at him with expectant eyes, he continued saying, "I guess you just want me to spill it hunh? No 'what?' from you?"

"If you don't just tell me why else you're really happy…" Her words tapered off as she stared at him. She didn't have a threat to verbalize to him, but she was counting on her stern look to command him to speak.

"Well," he flattened his palms against the small of her back, "I'm happy that my momma and your Nana were bossy enough to make me a bachelor at the end of that night. It's what finally brought us together after all these years. We've been going strong since that night." He could no longer hold back from kissing her naturally lined and plump lips, he licked his full, pink lips before he swooped down and pulled her bottom lip into his mouth.

She moaned as she massaged his neck, sending him into a frenzy as cupped her butt and squeezed it all the while gliding his tongue in and out and round her mouth as he savored her taste.

Remembering he had something else he wanted to say, he tried to pull away from her but her biting his bottom lip to keep him from pulling away made him smile against her lips. "I need to tell you something," he mumbled against her lips.

The rumbling of his lips against hers made her grin and she released his lip.

"What do you need to tell me?" She tilted her head at him.

"That I'm happy, blessed that you've been by my side every step of the way with opening up this place." He tucked her wavy hair behind her ear before he pulled on her lobe. "You are an amazing," his hand slid down to butt until he had an ample handful in each, "wonderful, smart, beautiful woman with a heart of gold and I love you."

Her eyes widened. "You what?" She held her breath wondering if he would repeat himself or pretend as if he hadn't said it.

"I love you," he said the words louder and stared into her eyes, hopefully leaving no room for mishearing or confusion on her part. "Ima, I love you."

Her eyes glossed over as her mouth widened into a full-face smile. "I love you too, baby." She jumped up in his arms and wrapped her arms tightly around his neck.

He chuckled as he held her in his arms and rubbed her back. Her sniffles alerted him to her crying.

When she loosened her hold on his neck, he placed

her back down on her feet but kept her close to him as she interlaced their hands. "Is it really surprising that I love you?"

"No, I mean with the way we've been going, I'm always at your place, the conversations we have digging more into each other's lives, even the quiet moments we spend together just holding hands, laying next to each other at night, the way you look at me when we wake up together, I could tell that you love me, it's just everything," she sighed a refreshing breath, "to hear you actually say the words. I've wanted to be with you so long." She bit the inside of her jaw as a tear fell from her eye.

He pulled her closer to him and lightly rubbed her face with the pad of his thumb.

"Like I told you, I liked you when I was younger, I just never thought the feeling was mutual, so I let it go. And over the years, with still thinking I'd never have a shot with you, plus the distance between us, and then you being married at one point, no disrespect, but I didn't give there ever being something between you and I much thought like that. But these past six months and dammit, you always wearing my favorite color on you, yellow," he kissed her exposed shoulder and her face glowed, "you just being you, so loving, attentive, helpful, I'd be a fool not to search myself enough to not know that I love you.

"And oh, I got you something." He lifted off the desk, pushing her away slightly to get past her and go behind his desk to grab something.

She suspiciously eyed the box wrapped in yellow wrapping paper and a pretty, white bow as he gripped it with both hands and came back to stand in front of her.

"Here, this is for you."

"What is it?"

"It's a gift. Open it up and see."

"A gift for me on the opening night for your restaurant?"

"Like I said, with the way you've helped me to coordinate this opening, improving my décor and design ideas, becoming my marketing guru and getting word out about this place, supporting me and calming me when we were behind on construction for a while, cooking and bringing me food the nights I stayed here late, this is just as much your opening as it is mine. We're a team. So yes, that's a gift for you tonight. Now open it woman." He chuckled as he placed it in her hands.

She smiled wide as she shimmied past him to place the big box on his desk. When she lifted the top of it, she frowned.

He laughed.

"What is this?" She pulled the yellow black apron and chef's hat out the box and held it up for him to see.

"It's an outfit."

"Jeremy," her voice squeaked, "I'm not the cook between the two of us. How is this get up for me?"

"Because, I want you to wear it tonight."

"Tonight? I know I told you that I would help you anyway I can here, but I don't think you want me in your kitchen. I know you say you like my cooking, but I'm no chef."

"I didn't say you had to wear it here."

"But you said tonight." Her brows lifted as her lips

poked out, staring at him in confusion.

"Tonight, after we close this place down. You didn't even see the other gift in there." He reached into the box and grabbed a spatula.

She chuckled as she snatched it from him. "Really? So I guess I'm supposed to smack you with this?"

"Actually, I'll be using that on you." He winked.

"You are so silly." She tapped his arm.

He reached into the bigger box and pulled out a smaller one. "Here."

She quickly grabbed it from him and opened it. It held two keys on a keychain. Rather than asking what they were for, she dangled them in front of him.

He laughed as he grabbed and kissed the back of her proffered hand. "I was thinking that," his hands dropped to her backside and he pulled her flush to him, "you could use those," he motioned his head to her hand holding the keys, "to let yourself into our place tonight."

"Our place?"

"Yeah, I want you to move in with me."

Her eyes widened.

"And, and I was thinking that you wear that tonight to celebrate these new beginnings for us."

"So you want me to put an apron and hat on with my pajamas?"

"No, I just want you to put the apron and hat on, nothing else. I know chefs normally wear them, but you won't need to cook anything tonight. You'll be my late night snack. Scratch that, I'm always hungry for you. You'll be my seven course meal and I'm ready to feast."

Gripping her ass with a fierceness, her legs instinctively wrapped around his waist as he lifted her and engaged her in a delectable kiss.

Escapades of Mama Peaches & Geraldine

Through monthly episodes some months back, Book Euphoria introduced the ladies who inspired the series, Mama Peaches and her partner in crime, Geraldine.

Mama Peaches is known as the "Mama of Chicago." Everyone knows her and to know her is to love her. To continue the initiative that her late husband started, Mama Peaches decides to lead the Southlake Park, IL restoration project to rebuild the community.

I authored the episodes of Peaches and Geraldine's escapades so that you could get to know the feisty ladies prior to the release of the Distinguished Gentlemen Series, but you may be reading these after you've read some of the bachelors' books.

There are four episodes included. Please enjoy.

Episode 1

Mama Peaches & Geraldine at City Council Meeting

"Girl, some of these men in here look like they just walked off the set of the Black Panther movie. Good Lawd he fine," Ms. Geraldine said, peering at a man not too far from where she and Mama Peaches were seated.

Mama Peaches turned fully in her seat to see who Geraldine was ogling. "Geraldine, that's why nothing with you has lasted. You pick the wrong ones." She turned back around and swatted her best friend's hands. "That man is probably barely fifty."

"And?"

"And you couldn't keep up with his tail even if you wanted to."

"I beg your pardon?" Geraldine's head reared back. "For one, you do know these teeth are removable, don't you?" Geraldine winked and made a slurping sound.

Mama Peaches buckled over with laughter. Wheezing, she sat up straight and wiped her eyes of the tears she shed from laughing so hard. "You are a fool, I tell ya. A fool."

"Call me what you will, but I'll be a satisfied fool. Fifty is just fine by me. He still has spring in his chicken if you know what I mean." She nudged Mama Peaches for confirmation.

"You better not say anything to that man that could jeopardize us getting the money we need to revitalize this neighborhood."

"See, you're looking at it all wrong. By the time I get done putting it on him," she swiveled her hips in a circle in her seat, "we'll have enough money to rehab Southlake Park and every other run-down neighborhood in the city."

With pursed lips, Mama Peaches leaned back to stare at her friend. "Geraldine, you can't ever keep your wig on straight, let alone put 'it' on him, as you say."

"Peaches!" The high pitch in Geraldine's voice drew attention to them from those close by. "You mean to tell me I've been sitting here all this time with my wig on backwards and you didn't bother to tell me?" She cut her eyes at Peaches.

"I was about to before you started talking about what you'd do to Fifty."

"You know what…" Geraldine's mouth tightened, and her eyes narrowed as she stared at Mama Peaches. "I ain't studying you." She rolled her eyes, snatched her purse from the seat next to her, and hung her head as she rushed to the bathroom.

Mama Peaches' hand flew up to her mouth as she snickered and watched Geraldine walk and hold her wig down as if it were a hat and a strong wind was trying to take it away.

Episode 2

Mama Peaches & Geraldine Go to The Salon

"Peaches, where are you taking me?" Geraldine asked, eyeing the street lined with restaurants.

"To the salon." Mama Peaches continued looking straight ahead while driving.

"The salon? Why you getting your hair done again so soon? You just got it done Tuesday."

"No, we're getting yours done."

"Mines done?" Geraldine gasped and clutched her invisible pearls. "I don't need my hair done. My wig collection suits me just fine."

Ignoring the green light ahead, Mama Peaches slammed on the breaks and cocked her head in Geraldine's direction. "Suits you fine? Geraldine, it's the middle of a heat wave in Chicago, my air conditioner is broke on this old thang, but we can't roll your window down to get a decent breeze coming through here because the wig you think suits you fine won't stay pinned down with even the slightest breeze. You're going to the salon." Mama Peaches pulled off, shaking her head.

"Peaches, I said my current wig collection suits me just fine," Geraldine said through pinched lips. She grunted and folded her arms over her chest. Her crimson red bottom lip poked out.

"If you're referring to that questionable stash of wigs you keep getting from that Korean beauty supply up the street, then I beg to differ."

"Ain't nothing wrong with me shopping at the Beauty Bar for my hair. The owner and on-site wig specialist, Jen Li, knows what I like and gives me discounts."

"Specialist? Ain't nothing special about what she does to your head. More like a mess I tell ya. Now, I'mma take you to my girl and she's gonna hook you up with one of those lace front wigs since you love wearing other people's hair so much."

"Lace front? Why not a cotton front since it's so hot. It would keep me cooler." Geraldine's shoulders bounced as she chuckled at herself. When she looked over and didn't see Mama Peaches enjoying her joke, she squashed her laughter and pursed her lips. "Ain't that what I let you talk me into getting some years back when they first became popular? Shoot, I ain't getting no damn lace front. My edges haven't grown back since that incident." Geraldine rubbed at her hairline.

Mama Peaches chuckled to herself, reeling in the flashback of watching Geraldine take the lace front wig off only a day after it had been installed. "That girl told you before we left that shop what you needed to do when you were ready to take it off, but no, after one day, you complained that it was too tight and snatched it off. That wasn't the lace front's fault, that was yours." She turned the wheel to the right and then put the car in park.

"I ain't studying you, Peaches." Geraldine wiped sweat from her forehead.

"Anyway. We're here and you're getting something done to that head of yours." Peaches stepped out of the car and let out a deep breath, fanning herself and reaching back into the car for her pocketbook. She looked back over at Geraldine rubbing deodorant under her arms. "Maybe even let your natural hair show."

Geraldine snapped her neck at Mama Peaches. "If I plan to be buried in and with my wig collection, you think I'mma be caught alive without one?"

Mama Peaches shook her head and slammed her car door before making her way to the salon.

"Peaches? Hold on. Peaches," Geraldine whispered loudly, shuffling her feet fast and clasping her wig with both hands.

Mama Peaches looked back at Geraldine struggling to hold her wig down while balancing her heavy purse on her arm and said, "And that's why we're here." She pulled the salon door open.

"Mama Peaches," a crowd of women screamed.

"Dawn, your nine to five appointment is right behind me," Mama Peaches said and a burst of laughter erupted in the salon as the door closed.

Episode 3

Mama Peaches & Geraldine at the Gym

Sitting down on the hard bench, legs spread wide apart, Mama Peaches bent over to tie her gym shoes.

"Hey, Peaches," Geraldine said, squeezing past Peaches, practically electric sliding over to a locker. She placed her tote bag on a bench and then stood straight to smooth out her clothes.

Mama Peaches sat up straight and turned to look over at her friend. Her head immediately reared back. "Geraldine," she said in a high pitched, questioning voice.

"What?" Geraldine tilted her head at Mama Peaches.

She merely pointed at Geraldine.

"It's cute, ain't it?" Geraldine's giddy voice matched the shimmy in her hips as she spun to model her outfit for Mama Peaches. "I got it from the thrift store."

Peaches shook her head. "You stay missing the mark."

"How so?" Geraldine's thin, black drawn on eyebrow arched high in query.

Mama Peaches looked her up and down. "FILA on your shirt, Reebok, big and bold down those snug leggings you're wearing, Adidas on your feet,

Under Armour headband, knee-high Nike socks. Looks like you were so focused on buying brands that you bought the whole alphabet of designers."

Geraldine swatted at Mama Peaches. "I ain't studying you.

"You should be. That outfit is more suited for a younger woman, not you."

"I beg your pardon?" Geraldine spun around as fast as she could after she locked her locker. "It's too tight on you in all of the wrong places. Deen, the seat of those pants is clearly shaped like an upside-down heart, but your butt is shaped like an upside-down pear."

"Oh Peaches, you stay hatin' on me."

"Hatin'? I'm tryna help ya," Mama Peaches said, getting up from the bench.

"Yes, I said hatin'." Geraldine walked out of the locker cove they were in and over to a mirror. She leaned in as she twisted her wig so that the short bang aligned up just right across her forehead.

"Hatin' ain't it, hunny."

"So what I wasn't blessed with a bedonkadonk like you, but the one I've had all of these years has suited me just fine. I have three ex-husbands to verify it, too." Geraldine pursed her lips.

"Sure that ain't why they left?" Mama Peaches mumbled under her breath and chuckled as she stepped beside Geraldine to reapply her deep, burgundy lipstick.

Geraldine cut her eyes at Peaches. "I heard that. And don't ever forget, I left them, they didn't leave me. Besides, it's October and I have what," she held her dark, freckled right hand up to count her fingers and began mumbling, "the rest of this month, November, December, January, February, and oh March." She spoke louder when her count was done. "I have a little under six months to get this booty firm and right." She turned to look at her backside in the mirror.

"Deen, you'll need more than six months to turn that pineapple into some passion fruit." Mama Peaches tickled herself so much, she had to fan herself amidst her coughing spell.

Geraldine shook her head. "I will not be bothered with you, Peaches. Like I said, I have enough time to get this body in shape for that bachelor auction you thought of to help raise funds to restore our community. Shoot, I plan on snatching me a bachelor too," Geraldine said, walking off with an extra pep in her steps.

Mama Peaches propped one hand on her lean hip and the other on the countertop next to her. She cocked her head staring at her friend.

"Before you think about snatching a man, you might wanna snatch that wig into place on your head."

Geraldine hissed and flew back to the mirror as fast as she could to fix her lopsided wig.

***

"Deen, I'm certain that's not how that machine works," Mama Peaches said as she sat upright and pulled on the handles of the row machine she sat at.

"Hush, Peaches. I know exactly what I'm doing." She winked at Mama Peaches before she cleared her throat and turned to face the man next to her. "Can you help me? I just don't know how to work this silly thing," she said in such a girlish voice that Mama Peaches leaned in to see if indeed it was Geraldine who had spoken.

"Sure." The forty-something looking man stood, legs somewhat straddling Geraldine with his biceps bulging and pecs flexing as he guided her hands correctly over the handles of the seated bench press. "You have to grip them just right and then breathe through pushing forward, making sure you don't lock your elbows when you extend your arms out."

With him still braced in front of her, she followed his directions a few times over until he said, "I think you have the hang of it."

"Yes, the hang of it," she said as her eyes traveled south, just below his waist and lingered there before Mama Peaches hissed at her.

"Geraldine."

"Oh yes, I definitely have the hang of it." She looked back up at him.

He flashed her an awkward smile before he grabbed his gym bag from the machine near hers and scurried off.

Mama Peaches shook her head at a giggling Geraldine. Soon Geraldine turned her head and asked the same question to the latest muscle-bulging man that occupied the machine next to hers.

It became clear to Mama Peaches after a while that her dear friend was purposefully misusing equipment as a ruse to engage the fine men around them.

Three men later and healthy eyefuls of all that God had blessed them with, Geraldine laid on her back sweaty, pretending like she was struggling with and trying to get the most recent guy to help her with the weight of the bench press hovering over her.

Blinded by her sweat, she only had the deep sound of a man's voice to indicate he was her next prey.

"Need help there, sexy momma?" He braced his headphones around his neck and turned off the Walkman hoisted on his waist.

"Yes." She giggled as her arms voluntarily shook as she pressed the handles upward.

With his arms braced on her triceps, he stood behind her, helping her press up. "How many are you doing for each set?"

"I don't know. How many should I do?" Her voice was girlish.

"For you, if you're going lighter on the weights, I say twenty would be a good amount, but if you go heavier then maybe stop at twelve per set."

"Oh, that's good to know." Geraldine relished in his firm hold on her arms. He had big hands, too.

Mama Peaches stopped movement on her machine and simply stared at Geraldine. She wasn't sure but she would bet the five-dollar bill in her purse that Geraldine couldn't see the man's face through the sweat drenching hers and obviously dripping in her eyes. She had an unobstructed view of the man and couldn't wait for Geraldine to see what she was seeing. He was a sight to behold alright. She grabbed a Snickers from her fanny pack to enjoy the rest of the show.

"Whew. What was that, thirty-six times I did that?" Geraldine said with her eyes closed as the gentleman helped her sit upright.

"Yup. Thirty-six perfect times. You're a pro at this."

"Let me get the sweat out of my eyes so I can stand up and properly thank you." She smirked.

Mama Peaches fully turned her body to face Geraldine and bit into the last of her Snickers.

"Okay, but if it's not too much to ask, may I have your number? I'd love if we can meet here more often. I can help you work out and maybe take you out soon? You know, on a date?"

The sweetness and deep tenor of his voice coursed through Geraldine with an exhilaration that had her rushing to wipe her face with the towel hanging from her fanny pack. When her face was free of sweat and she had smoothed what was left of her eyebrows back in place, she turned to look at him, but stumbled as her hand flew up to her chest.

"You alright?" He rushed to her and held on to her hoping to help her keep her balance. "You know you have to stay hydrated when you work out and take your time when getting up, otherwise, you may get lightheaded like you just did."

"Yeah, yeah, lightheaded, that's it," Geraldine stammered, talking as she stepped back from his embrace.

Peaches sat nearby, hand covering her mouth trying to quell her laughter.

Geraldine shot her a deathly glare before she looked back at the man in front of her. She was struggling to make sense of it all. She shook her head as if it would erase the past moments. "I'm sorry, but was that you just helping me on that there bench?" She placed her hand over her chest for support of her well-being.

"Yes." He chuckled. I could see that you were sweating a lot, but I didn't know you couldn't see me at all." He winced and braced his hand on his lower back. "I'll be doing fine for a couple of days then old Arthur will show up again and try to shut me down. You know what I'm saying."

"No, I don't." Geraldine straightened her back and her chin lifted high.

"You know Arthur, arthritis. I'm sure at your age he's been paying you plenty of visits too." He chuckled.

Geraldine looked him up and down, giving him a cold look that made him freeze even the smallest of movements he had going.

"You know what," she said and tightened her lips as her eyes narrowed in on him. "I'mma go get that water you suggested." She turned to walk away but his voice slowed her movements.

"But there's a water bottle at your feet. I thought maybe we could go walk on the treadmills side by side, sort of act like we're taking a walk through the park and get to know one another better."

Her head snapped back. "Water I said. I'm going to get water." She kicked over the bottle at her feet as she rushed off into the locker room nearby.

"Excuse me," Mama Peaches said, snickering as discreetly as she could as she picked up Geraldine's water bottle from the floor and then went in search of her friend.

"Geraldine. Geraldine. Where are you?" Mama Peaches said, laughing as she passed two rows of lockers.

A dark hand snatched her into the folds of the third row of lockers.

"Deen," Mama Peaches yelped. "What are you doing?"

"Shhhh. Don't say my name out loud anymore. He may hear it. Is he behind you?" She slowly peeked her head out into the openness of the locker room.

"Deen, this is the women's locker room. Why would he follow you in here?"

"I don't know. You saw how sweet he was on me. Talking 'bout can we walk on the treadmills together as if we're walking through the park." She turned to look at Mama Peaches.

"Peaches, the man thinks rubber and grass looks alike." She popped the palm of her hand against her forehead as she shook her head. "The man ain't too bright." She went and took a seat next to Mama Peaches on the bench.

"Deen, you didn't come here to work out, you came here to get a man. The other ones you tried to snag dismissed you, but when a good one puts the moves on you, you blow him off? Sounds like you're missing your own point to me." Mama Peaches stood and unlocked her locker.

"Peaches, the other men were fine, virile, but that man, one who's clearly best friends with Arthur ain't my type."

"And why not?"

"For one he insulted me saying I was friends with Arthur. I'm just as youthful and as in great health as I want to be."

Peaches cocked her head. "So Arthur didn't have you bedridden last summer for two weeks?"

Geraldine thought on it for a second. "Oh hush." She waved off Mama Peaches.

Mama Peaches laughed as she took her tote bag from the locker and sat it on the bench behind her.

"And not only did he insult me, but Peaches, the man has no teeth." She shuddered.

"I saw that." Mama Peaches buckled over with laughter.

"I ain't studying you, Peaches." She finally went to her locker and struggled to fit the key in it properly. She paused to share more with the cackling hen next to her. "But the nail in his coffin was that Walkman."

Mama Peaches' forehead wrinkled. "What's wrong with him having a Walkman?"

Geraldine cocked her head in disbelief. "What do you mean what's wrong with him still having a Walkman? That thang is ancient and had duct tape on it to keep it all together."

Mama Peaches sniggered, remembering just how tattered the device looked on his hip.

Geraldine ignored Peaches' antics and continued. "He probably does everything the old way. Even make love the old way."

"Deen, what?"

"Peaches, don't act like you don't know what I'm talking about. Old married couples used to sleep in separate beds. You tell me how that was possible unless they was only doing it to make babies and not have any fun."

Peaches just stared at her.

"You know I ain't lying." She finally unlocked her locker. "Ain't no way they was doing the downward facing dog, sixty-nine, the tree lotus, and all these other new moves and able to keep they hands off each other." She pulled her bag from the locker and made her way towards the exit of the locker room. "Nope. I don't want no old dog using old tricks. Gonna get me a new, young one with new tricks."

"You ain't getting none to be worried about any of that," Mama Peaches said, close on her heels.

"You don't know what I'm getting," Geraldine tossed over her shoulder as she stepped back into the gym and was instantly greeted by the toothless man.

"Hey, got enough water in you now?"

Geraldine stepped back. He was too close to her for her liking.

"I was hoping I could catch you when you came back out. I'd really like to get your digits and take you out some time."

Trying to calculate her thoughts, Geraldine just stared at him.

Hoping to seal the deal with her, he leaned in and said, "And if you're worried about me not having any teeth, don't. I have a set in my gym bag. I took 'em out when I saw the fine fox that you are."

Her face scrunched.

"I just wanted you to see that my mouth works wonders without them if you know what I mean."

She jerked back as she gasped. She turned to face Mama Peaches and through clenched teeth said, "Peaches, let's go now." She brushed past him and took quick steps to get out of his view and out of the gym.

Mama Peaches had heard everything he said and had to hold on to one machine after another as her laughter crippled her so that she staggered out of the gym.

Episode 4

Mama Peaches & Geraldine's Bingo Attempt

"Deen, why you ain't been answering your phone?" Mama Peaches said, grabbing her purse from off the hook on the back of her bedroom door.

"Peaches, I don' messed up," Geraldine whispered, looking over to the left of her. She shivered in disgust before pulling the covers up closer to her neck and gripping the phone tighter.

"What are you talking about? And why are you so hush?" Mama Peaches locked her front door behind her. "You better not still be laying down when you know good and well you should be up and ready to go to the bingo hall with me."

"Peaches, I don't know about going to the bingo hall today. I don' messed up big time this time." Geraldine shuffled from her bed and wrapped the white sheet around her body. She lifted her hand to scratch her head, but feeling nothing but a stocking cap, she silently shrieked before she looked at the bed to see her Diana Ross-like wig near her pillow. She lurched forward and snatched it from the bed and slapped it on her head. She used the hand with the phone in it to hold it down while her other hand worked to stretch it out over her head.

Mama Peaches stopped in her tracks on her front porch steps and stared into the street as if Geraldine was in front of her and could see the frown lines on her forehead and slightly gaped mouth, but she wasn't. Only her late husband's 1973 Cadillac Deville—shiny and ready for her to drive—was in sight. She could only use words to communicate with her friend. "Deen, what is going on?"

"Well, remember when we went to that library on the west side to pass out flyers for the Bachelor Auction?"

"Yeah."

"And remember we stumbled upon those Book Euphoria girls that Saturday selling their books?" Geraldine narrowed her eyes, staring at her bed.

"Yeah, Deen. What does that have to do with anything?" Mama Peaches closed her car door.

"I've been hit by Madden Mania."

Mama Peaches was clueless as to what her friend was talking about as she started up the old school car.

"Peaches, I bought two books from that pretty girl with the long hair, you know the one that liked to hug."

"Okay, and?" Mama Peaches remembered exactly which one Geraldine was referring to.

"Well, she had some books about brothers, and I bought them. Peaches, the way she described that man in Blessed by Malakai... She had me fanning myself down there like it was a fiery furnace."

When the recognition of what Geraldine was saying hit Mama Peaches, she shook her head. "Deen."

"Peaches, I ain't lying. I had fans blowing on me from every which direction trying to get my hotbox's temperature back to normal."

Frustrated with Geraldine's antics, Mama Peaches sighed. "What does any of this have to do with you whispering on the phone right now and probably not ready for bingo? You know I hate to be late."

"That's what I'm trying to tell you, but I had to start from the beginning. I should've known better not to fool with that girl's books after that first one, but I just couldn't help myself. Those Madden Men keep you wanting more, so I started reading the next book in the series last night."

Mama Peaches stopped at a red light. "Are you saying you've been in bed all day because you were up all night reading?"

"I was up all night reading, but that ain't what has me whispering and not ready yet."

"Well, what is it, Deen?" The light turned green and Mama Peaches put her foot on the gas again.

"Are you gonna let me tell you, or you just gon' keep interrupting me?" Geraldine bucked her neck as if Mama Peaches could see her.

Mama Peaches pursed her lips as she made a right turn.

"Peaches, I thought that first book about Malakai was something else, but that damn Crayson Madden made my pocketbook cray cray for real."

Mama Peaches slammed on her breaks. Luckily, no one was behind her. "Deen, what the hell are you telling me?"

"Hold on Peaches."

"Deen!" Mama Peaches screamed into the Bluetooth around her neck.

Geraldine didn't respond to Mama Peaches but rather made her way around to the other side of her bed and poked who she'd left in it.

He rolled over and stretched.

She cringed, squeezing her eyes shut at the sight in front of her before she started grabbing the clothes near her feet and throwing them at him.

He sat up smiling and trying to speak, but her eyes widened as her pointer finger flew up to her mouth, signaling him to be quiet. Her lips tightened and her nostrils flared.

He got the picture and grinned as he sat up and began to get dressed.

Geraldine grabbed the robe hanging near her bedroom door, put it on, and stepped into the hallway.

She stepped a few paces away from the bedroom door before she turned her attention back to Mama Peaches on the phone. "What I'm trying to tell you, if you would just let me get the rest of the story out, is by the time that Crayson had finish sexing that girl in her secret room, I was drenched down there. You hear me? Drenched. I had to get a towel to clean myself up before I got in the shower. I was still so hot and bothered when I got out the shower that I figured going to the gym would help me since they say you release them dolphins when you exercise."

Mama Peaches' face scrunched as she mouthed "dolphins" several times. Still not grasping what Geraldine was saying, she asked, "What? Dolphins live in the ocean."

"Naw, you know, them things that make you happy. Them dolphins."

"You mean endorphins?"

"That's what I said, them dolphins."

Mama Peaches didn't even bother to correct her friend.

With silence on the other end, Geraldine continued her story, "I was at the gym working out, trying to relieve that built up tension the men in them books created down there, but it just wasn't working." Growing hot all over again, Geraldine shook her head. "And then I saw him."

As if she had summoned him, he emerged from her room, smiling and walking towards her with his arms wide, to embrace her.

"Saw who?" Mama Peaches asked, finally pulling up to Geraldine's house.

"Him, Peaches," Geraldine said, swatting his hands away from her and walking backward until they were near her front door.

He didn't let up on trying to embrace her as he stepped behind her and wrapped his arms around her. His puckered lips teased the sweet spot behind her ears.

Between the images of what the Madden Men had done to the women in the books, remembering his tongue reaching way past his chin when he stuck it out, and the kisses he currently trailed on her neck, she was losing all sensibility. "Peaches, oh Peaches…" Her words came out in the combination of a moan and a grunt, remembering the scenes from the books as well as her afternoon activities. She cleared her throat as his arms wrapped tighter around her. "Peaches, you remember Walkman Man." She found the strength to pull from his embrace and open her front door.

"What is with all of this remembering you have me doing?" Mama Peaches said.

"Peaches?" Geraldine's dark brown eyes widened when the door was fully opened.

"What, Deen?" Mama Peaches said, looking past Geraldine and staring directly into Walkman Man's face.

He smiled, toothless, as he nodded his head at Mama Peaches. He leaned in and kissed Geraldine on her cheek. He squeezed her butt for kicks, to which she jumped, and then he walked out the front door.

Stunned, Mama Peaches' head turned to follow him before she looked back at Geraldine.

"Walkman Man from the gym," Geraldine said into her phone.

"Deen, I'm in your face. Hang up the phone," Mama Peaches scolded.

Geraldine was so flustered that she struggled to press the End button. When she looked up at Mama Peaches, she couldn't read her facial expression, so she pulled her robe tighter around her and said, "Now wait a minute, don't you judge me." She wagged her finger at Mama Peaches.

"I'm not judging you." Peaches chuckled to herself and clutched her purse tighter. "I'm just saying that after all that talk about him never being able to get near you that you... you..." she studied the glow and embarrassment on her friend's face and said, "let him get so close to you."

Geraldine covered her face with both hands before she quickly dropped them and her eyes and mouth widened as she stared at Mama Peaches. One hand flew up to her hip and all her weight shifted to that one side of her body. "I know, right? After the first time I met him, if someone would've told me that he and I would, you know, I would've had them committed to a looney bin. But Peaches, the man didn't have his teeth in again today. I was so bothered, and when he saw me, he wasted no time in showing me how far the tip of his tongue went past his chin." She gripped her robe tightly. "Peaches, he touched my soul with that thang."

Mama Peaches shivered. "Deen, I don't want to hear that." She shooed Geraldine to turn. "Just get in there and get ready so we can go." She stepped forward to walk in the house, but Geraldine turning back to face her halted her steps.

"Just one more thing." Geraldine's pulse sped up.

"What?" Mama Peaches' tone was sharp as she folded her arms under her breasts.

"I was wrong." Geraldine squealed.

"About what?"

"Him, Peaches. That old dog is young at heart, mouth, stamina, and everything else you can name."

Mama Peaches shook her head and shooed her friend into her house.

Geraldine walked but talked loudly over her shoulder. "I'm serious, Peaches. I thought the kind of stuff he did to me only happens in those romance novels. But boy does that old dog have some great," she licked her lips, "tricks up his sleeve. Oooh," she flailed her arms, "let me go take a cold shower before I have to call him back over here."

"And fix your wig while you're at it." Peaches shook her head as she closed the door behind her.

DISTINGUISHED GENTLEMEN

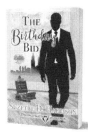
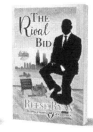

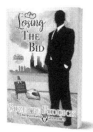

Other Books Available

<u>Sisterhood Chronicles Series</u>
Underneath It All
Discovery
Untold
When It Happens To You
All Things Considered

<u>Forever Friends Series</u>
Catch Me If You Can
It's Complicated

<u>Limelight Series</u>
Hues
Tones

<u>Standalone Titles</u>
After All Is Said & Done

(Best if you read Forever Friends series before reading Sisterhood Chronicles 3)

COMING SOON

Vision: Limelight 3
The Kissing Game: Love Alive 1

ABOUT THE AUTHOR

Anita Davis is a former elementary teacher born and raised in Chicago. Although she wrote short stories much of her childhood, she didn't unlock and cultivate her passion as a writer until she became a writing teacher for middle school students. The more she had to create sample writings for her students, the more she realized her passion and ability to tell stories in the written form. She decided to hone her craft as a writer by completing her Master of Fine Arts in Creative Writing via National University. She now pursues writing books most of her time, in addition to being a flight attendant. Anita seeks to encourage, engage, and entertain her readers.

authoranitadavis@gmail.com
www.authoranitadavis.com
Facebook: Anita Davis and Author page: Author Anita Davis
Instagram: @authoranitadavis   Twitter: @_AnitaDavis
Subscribe to mailing list: Anita's Newsletter

Made in the USA
Middletown, DE
02 June 2019